The Ice Dragon

A Christmas Tale

Daisy Parkin

To Zoe and Ross for the joy of Christmas past, present and future.

Contents

Ice

Ice crawls along the path
across the lawn.
It hangs on trees
and spiders' webs.
It casts a wicked spell,
turning locks frozen.
Ears blushing red,
noses, fingers, toes.

Ice crackles like meringue
beneath my feet.
Slides hump-back hills
glides rocky steps.
It shuts snails tight in shells
pours varnish on roofs,
drips candy floss
patterns on windows.

It spins. It spins glittering thread
to bind the earth
with magic strands
of molten glass.
The rooks look to the North
they shiver.
When will the ice come?

Chapter 1. The Journey

Katy stared moodily out of the train window, a frown etched between her dark brown eyes. It was hard to see anything as the glass was steamed up, but she could hear the waves crashing against the sea wall close to the railway tracks. She was on her way to her grandparents' home in Devon, it was the middle of December, close to Christmas, but she had to go on her own. Lucy, her mum's friend, was going down to see her own family in Dartmouth so she had offered to take Katy with her as far as Torquay. Katy's grandparents would meet her at the station there.

'Come on love, don't fret,' Lucy patted Katy's hand. 'Your sister will be fine.'

Katy's sister Ruthie was in hospital after an accident. Her parents were staying with Ruthie and hoping to come down later in December, but nothing was definite.

Katy felt miserable, normally she would love to be going to see her grandma and grandpa, but now? She wasn't sure. The wind threw rain against the window, and buffeted the carriage which rocked like a giant cradle. The weather reflected her own emotions which were in turmoil, perhaps the waves would wash the train into the sea and she wouldn't have to explain anything to anyone ever again.

She tried to concentrate on her book, impatiently flicking her hair, a tangle of red curls, over her shoulder, but her mind drifted away to that awful day when Ruthie had been hurt. 'No, don't think about it,' she said to herself.

'Don't think about it.'

Just then her attention was taken by a little boy two rows down from her standing on his seat wielding a sticky, orange lollipop in a grubby, tiny hand. He seemed to be brushing the hair of the man sat in front of him with it, whom she assumed must be asleep. All of a sudden there was a howl as the child realised his sugar laden treat was now well and truly stuck to the man's head. The man turned around, a drop of sleep drool rolled down to his chin, the lollipop was swinging from side to side, dangling from a long bit of ginger hair which until now had been covering a bald patch.

'What the …????' The man's eyes bulged unbecomingly as he glared at the tearful child. Undeterred the little boy continued to yank at his sweet, until his mother gabbed his arm.

'I am so sorry,' she apologised. 'Please let me help you.' She reached out to disentangle the lollipop.

'Do not touch me!' the man grunted, with no attempt to be polite. With some difficulty he tore the lollipop from his hair and handed it back to the boy, who obligingly plunged it back into his mouth.

'Oh dear,' the mother said ineffectually.

Katy's eyes slid back to her book, her lips slightly curling at the edges.

Eventually the train glided into the station and slowed down by the platform. The wind was blowing the signs standing by the red and green painted entrance to the station café. One said: "Come to see Father Christmas at Cockington Court!" Another was advertising Costa Coffee. They creaked and rattled as the wind whistled

carelessly down the train track. Steam billowed out of the café door as it swung open and Katy's grandma emerged, wearing a bright cherry-coloured coat, an enormous smile on her face, her hair swept up into a grey-peppered bun. She spotted Katy following Lucy out of the carriage door and waved at her. Katy couldn't help noticing the slight nod her grandma gave to Lucy. An action that left her heart sinking.

'Thank you so much for bringing Katy with you. We're so grateful.'

Lucy smiled at Grandma Rose. 'Honestly it's been no

trouble at all, I was coming down anyway - it was lovely to have the company.' She hugged Katy. 'Bye my love, don't worry it will all work out.'

She glanced at the taxi rank where the drivers were waiting impatiently for fares. 'Well have a wonderful Christmas and I shall keep in touch to see if you need help getting home again Katy.'

'Thank you,' Grandma Rose answered for Katy as she took her bag and looped her arm through Katy's.

They stood together waving Lucy off as her taxi pulled away. Grandma's car stood near the taxi rank, it was green and shiny like a rose beetle. She opened the boot and popped Katy's travel bag inside whilst Katy slid into the front of the car and put her seat belt on. Rain flung itself onto the bonnet and streamed from the roof. As Grandma battled to join Katy, the wind howled like a wounded animal eager to push past her, blowing the car park ticket from the dashboard to the floor. With some difficulty she closed the door. She stretched across and kissed Katy on the cheek.

'Well maid, your grandpa can't wait to see you, we've got you all to ourselves for a change.'

Katy was surprised, she had expected to be asked the usual questions about Ruthie, the ones she didn't want to answer. She gave a glimmer of a smile. But she didn't trust herself to speak.

Grandma started up the engine and the car pulled off, battling the storm. The day was beginning to give way to an early dusk and, as they passed shops and houses, lights twinkled from Christmas trees in windows. Some houses were lit up outside too with garish, flickering snowmen or Father Christmases, bravely daring the weather to dowse their brilliance.

In twenty minutes they were at the house. It was large and ramshackle, the front door had seen better days, but when it opened there was a lovely aroma of dinner cooking. Grandpa appeared wearing an apron covered in pink roses and holding a large spoon, which he promptly dropped by the oven hob as he came to greet them. 'Hello my luvver! How's my bobby dazzler then?'

'Ok.' Katy mumbled.

Grandma glanced at Grandpa. 'I think this young lady is pretty tired, bless her. Let's get this bag up to your bedroom ready to unpack and then we'll have dinner. Cottage pie isn't it Ron?' Grandpa nodded.

'But first let's have a good look at you Katy, we're so pleased to see you.' Grandpa gave Katy such a bear hug the breath was knocked from her body. They did seem happy to see her, but did they really know what had happened, perhaps they wouldn't be so delighted if they really knew. She was afraid to relax ...... did they know?

The furniture in her bedroom was very old. The doors of the wardrobe were carved with flowers and small creatures that glowed in the mellow sheen of aged, solid wood. She had nearly always gone to sleep staring at it when staying with her grandparents, trying to count all the little mice or nodding bluebells whittled out of the oak. The room's window overlooked a large garden, very overgrown at the bottom, where there also stood Grandpa's workshop, which was really just a big shed. An old apple tree grew in the middle with one or two leaves still clinging to it in desperation against the frantic gusts of wind. In the darkness it looked like the hand of a giant sprung from the earth. A bay hedge surrounded the garden, a castle wall defying all invaders. Katy sighed and wondered how she would get through the next few weeks. She closed the curtains and went downstairs to dinner.

The next morning the storm had blown itself out. A still dreaming sun peeped drowsily from the haze of a wintry mist. Katy pulled the bedcovers over her head despite the fact her alarm clock clearly showed it was already 9 am. What was there to get up for?

'There you go my dear.' Grandma Rose put a cup of tea down next to Katy's bed. 'Did you sleep well?'

Katy muttered something non-committal from below the eiderdown.

'Breakfast in half an hour, slug-a-bed!' Grandma Rose chuckled.

Katy's tousled head appeared momentarily. 'Is there any eggy bread?'

'Of course, but only if you're up in time!' Grandma Rose went out humming to herself, collecting Katy's clothes from the floor to put in the wash.

After breakfast Katy went out into the garden to see her Grandpa Ron who was tut-tutting over large holes in his lawn.

'Them bloomin' badgers.' He surveyed the ground with dismay. 'And look at that!' He pointed to a patch of earth where flower bulbs had been dug up, some of them half eaten.

'How do they get in?' asked Katy.

'Through that there fencing,' replied her Grandpa pointing to a gap in the wire dividing his garden from the garden next door. 'I keep mending it, but badgers are powerful beasts, you don't want to get into a fight with a badger.'

He looked dolefully at a small hedgehog house tucked under the bay hedge. 'Not seen one hedgehog since the badgers started getting in.' Katy felt a pang as there had always been one particular hedgehog they called Henry who used to come out into the garden at night, snuffling for insects and worms.

'Ah well,' he continued philosophically 'badgers have to live like all creatures.'

The garden was still full of colour, hellebores and winter flowering jasmine brightened the banks, whilst pots and hanging baskets were adorned with deep purple pansies and shy violas. A winter clematis trailed over the wall waving its white bells, dancing in the gentle breeze. Grandpa Ron started to dig the bulbs back into the heavy, wet earth, a small robin flew to the handle of his garden fork its red breast bursting with song. 'Good morning' it seemed to sing, 'it's quite a good one don't you think?'

It then flew off to the bird bath, which was filled to the brim from yesterday's rain and proceeded to dowse itself, scattering water drops onto an unsuspecting squirrel digging up acorns nearby. Katy couldn't help herself, she laughed, the noise was so unexpected Grandpa glanced up and grinned. The squirrel turned to her then scampered off, but the robin was intent on its bathing and ignored her.

'Are you going to help me then maid?' Grandpa asked Katy. She picked up a trowel thrusting it into the soft ground, breathing in the rich, damp smell of the earth which promised next year's harvest. She took the delicate bulbs, some of which had already sprouted tiny leaves and gently laid them, right side up in the ground. As she was working in the corner of the garden she noticed a small tree standing by Grandpa Ron's workshop.

'That's new isn't it?'

Grandpa smiled, 'Yes, it's a conifer, it comes from a very cold region I think. Of course, I've lost the information label!'

Katy went over to it, she felt the deep-green needled branches which were surprisingly soft, near the top was a small cluster of pine cones, to her astonishment they were a violet blue hue. 'I've never seen any cones this colour before, aren't they beautiful?'

'Yes, I just hope that squirrel doesn't decide to eat them, I believe they quite like pine cones, especially for their Christmas dinner!'

The cones were closed up tightly, she knew that when they became bigger and began to open they would shed nuts which were really seeds. Sometimes her mother would buy pine nuts in the supermarket for cooking, but she supposed they might come from a different type of tree. She stroked the soft, feathery tendrils, somehow it was soothing, the tang of pine smelt of Christmas and all the excitement which came with it, the candles lit, the stockings hung for gifts, the decorating of the tree and the carol singing. Of course there wouldn't be snow, there hardly ever was, especially here. Not like on the thousands of Christmas cards which were sold every year. But there was the robin. Katy watched as the robin stood on the edge of the bird bath fluffing its feathers, full of self-importance. It cocked its head to one side, fixing Katy with a stare, daring her to come closer.

'I call that cheeky chap Bert, he's fearless. I've seen him fight off birds twice his size for a nice juicy worm unfortunate enough to stick its head out of the ground.' Grandpa chuckled. 'You have to get up early to get the better of him!'

The robin fluttered onto the pine tree, undaunted by Katy, it had spotted something crawling along one of the branches which it obviously fancied for its morning snack.

Katy watched closely, what had it seen? Along a twig close to her a tiny silver caterpillar was edging its way from one of the blue fir cones. The segments of its body shone in the watery sunlight and sparkled, enticing the hungry robin ever closer. It hopped from branch to branch and if robins had lips Katy was sure it would have been licking them. She was fascinated wondering when the robin would pounce, but suddenly she felt sorry for the little caterpillar and with one swift movement scooped it up into her hand.

The robin trilled with indignation.

'Sorry Bert, try the bird table,' Katy was unrepentant, cupping the silver caterpillar in her hand she walked slowly to the kitchen door. She would find a jam jar to put it in and make some holes in the lid. What was a caterpillar doing in the garden at this time of year anyway? How very odd. Surely the middle of winter wasn't the best time for it to be out?

Grandma was bustling about cooking bread and small banana and chocolate muffins in the oven. The steam from the stew pan where she was cooking lunch misted the kitchen windows, despite the extractor fan whirring away. Flour clung to the end of her nose and sprinkled her apron. The smell was delicious.

'Well my dear, what can I do for you then?' she enquired dusting flour from her hands.

'Do you have an empty jar Grandma?'

'What do you want it for Katy?'

'Well, this caterpillar.' answered Katy. She opened her hand, the motion of the caterpillar tickled as, clearly puzzled, it seemed to go round in circles.

'Oh my!' exclaimed Grandma Rose. 'What on earth is a caterpillar doing roaming the garden at this time of year! Of course you can have a jar, but you need to put something inside to make it feel at home. And don't forget to make holes in the lid.' Katy found an old jar in the larder Grandma had kept to make jam, it was quite large, so she was able to fit several baby pine cones into it and a small holly twig. The caterpillar wriggled out of her hand onto the cones and tucked itself away. She took the jar upstairs into her bedroom, and popped it on a small table next to her bed. As she examined her new discovery, down below the doorbell rang followed by the sound of voices.

'Hello Freddie, how are you today?' She heard her grandma say. 'Come in, come in, she's just upstairs.'

The door to Katy's bedroom opened and there appeared a skinny boy with a mop of curly black hair. His glasses sitting on his nose looked far too big for his face, but underneath them was the broadest grin you could imagine, punctuated by two dimples either side.

Katy smiled, really smiled, for the first time in days.

'Hi Katy.'

'Hi Freddie.' Without further ado Freddie plonked himself down on the bed and picked up the jar that was lying on the table.

'What have you got here then Kat? Another one of your pets? You always used to have something you were looking after from the garden.'

'Not really, it's just a caterpillar.'

Freddie stared into the jar, twisting it around in his hand. 'Are you sure Kat? I can't see anything.' He put it down and turned to Katy. 'How's Ruthie?' He asked without any hesitation or awkwardness. They had all known one another for so long, having grown up playing in each other's houses and going to school together until her father had made them move up north for his job a few years ago, and it didn't seem strange that he should be the one to ask and she would be the one not to mind.

'Well, it was a bad fall, she was in hospital for a while as it completely knocked her out and her leg was broken in two places.'

'What happened?'

'Freddie,' Katy looked at her friend dismally, 'it was my fault, we were mucking around and I pushed her too high on the swing. The chain broke and she went flying onto the concrete, I don't think mum and dad will ever really forgive me ...... and as for Ruthie.' She became silent and then she said it. 'What if she can never dance again?'

Katy searched Freddie's face for some sort of reaction. No one could blame her more than she blamed herself, it did her good to finally get it out into the open, the thing she was scared of, how she could never take back what had happened and how she was afraid things would never be the same again between her and Ruthie or between herself and her parents. How could anyone else forgive her when she couldn't forgive herself?

'Kat it was an accident. Don't you think there are things we would all like to wish away? You can't have known the swing would break, it could just as easily have been you sitting on it and Ruthie pushing it.' He stared at her through his glasses like a wise old owl.

'I know, if only it had been.' Katy replied.

Grandma's voice floated up the stairs, 'Are you staying to lunch Freddie?'

Freddie's eyes lit up, 'Ooooh yes please Mrs Clutter-buck, it smells so good and Mum's at the hospital working her shift till 7pm. It beats peanut butter sandwiches!'

He poked a finger at the jar. 'I wonder when I shall get to see your mystery guest!'

He started to laugh. 'Talking about mysteries, have you met Mr Entwhistle yet? He's had that monster house built next door to your grandparents, while he's been travelling around the world for the last two years looking for some other gruesome creature to be discovered. He found that leech a few years ago, do you remember?' Freddie shivered, 'Who'd want to discover a rotten old leech anyway, all they do is suck your blood.'

'Well they might be useful for something else,' Katy tried to be fair. 'I mean they must be on the planet for some reason. You know, ecosystems and stuff.'

'Yes, I s'pose it might be worth it if they were the staple diet for a lesser spotted pink parrot or something.'

'Or a hippo used them for eyebrows.' They looked at each other and grinned.

Later that evening before Katy went to sleep she decided to check on the caterpillar. Eventually, twisting the jar this way and that, the light caught what looked like a small, silver chrysalis clinging to one of the strange blue fir cones. 'Well there won't be much to see there for a while,' she thought, 'it'll takes ages before it hatches into a butterfly and then I shall set it free, funny little thing.'

She yawned, at least the news from her parents that night about Ruthie had been better. She did miss her sister. The bed felt warm and snug. There was a small chink in the bedroom curtains and through it the moon gazed down serenely. Katy stared back at it, her eyelids growing heavier as she thought about Ruthie, until eventually she fell asleep.

The next few days were very busy. Grandma Rose and Grandpa Ron were getting things ready for Christmas and as they were expecting Katy's mum, dad and Ruthie to join them they were pulling out all the stops. Freddie was still at school until the end of the week, he was quite jealous about Katy being able to "skive off" as he put it, as he was counting the days on his calendar until the school holidays.

Grandpa took her to the Christmas tree farm which lay on the way to Totnes. It was very busy as usual on the lead up to the festivities. The farm had a shop full of Christmas decorations to buy, a grotto to meet Santa and a café where you could enjoy things like tea, hot chocolate, scones, crumpets and tea cakes. Having found a parking space they jumped out of the car, luckily they were both wearing wellies, as the fields were muddy and squelchy after all the rain during the last few days, and deep puddles awaited them. Winter gales had struck again, tearing at leafless branches and tiled roofs, the rain cascading down from gutters into overflowing drains in the roads. But now the day had dawned fresh and cold, the sun weakly smiling from the sky whilst the world tried to shake off its sodden mantle. Katy and Grandpa Ron roamed up and down the avenues of fir trees still planted in the earth, some huge and towering, some much smaller and daintier. There were such a variety of types, Serbian Spruces, Blue Spruces, Fraser Firs, and Norway Spruces, too many, or so it seemed to Katy, to choose from. Their branches of various green hues danced joyfully in the slight breeze coming across from the distant

21

moors, the previous night's rain glistening, like beads of pearl, upon them.

'Now Grandma isn't fond of hoovering up bits of Christmas tree, so I think we need to look for a Nordmann Fir Katy, it won't drop its needles so much.'

The house Katy's grandparents lived in was quite old, the ceilings were higher than in many newer houses, so they were looking for something about twelve feet tall. After another twenty minutes they stopped in front of "the tree". Everyone knows when they find the right Christmas tree for them. It certainly looked a good height for the house, the trunk was straight and the silhouette was perfect, lower down, like a full green crinoline, it blossomed into the ideal shape. Grandpa spotted a ticket hanging on it.

'Oh dear, I think we'll have to forget this one Katy. It looks like someone has already bought it.'

Katy couldn't help feeling disappointed, it had felt as if the tree had been beckoning them all the while, but now she realised it had just been teasing them. It belonged to someone else, not to them. There was a gentleman standing a little further on, he turned at Grandpa's words.

'Can I help you?' he asked them. 'I work here, were you interested in that tree?'

'Well yes,' answered Grandpa Ron, 'but it has a reserved ticket on it.'

'Ah, all may not necessarily be lost,' answered the man, 'she is a beauty isn't she? I think we can do something about that.'

He walked over to the tree, his boots squelching in the soft mud. He picked up the ticket dangling from one of the branches.

'Oh,' he said, 'you do have good taste. This is one of the trees reserved for the Queen.'

'In that case I don't think we should have it,' Katy blurted out a little nervously, already feeling a hand on her collar dragging her off to the Tower. The man grinned.

'That's fine, we can find another one to send to the royal household, we send a lot to them. This tree spoke to you and you should have it.' He took the ticket off the branch and gave it to Katy. It had "Windsor Great Park" written on it with the picture of a crown printed above the words.

'Here, just to prove to your friends you have one of the Queen's trees.' Katy beamed at him in surprise, 'Thank you!'

He put another ticket on it and wrote their name on it. 'I expect you'll want this delivered, it's a little bigger than normal.'

They trudged back to the farm shop where grandpa arranged for their Nordmann Fir to arrive after cutting, luckily it would be the next day. Katy meanwhile went to look at the Christmas ornaments which were displayed in trays or hanging from small trees. There were baubles of every colour and every shade imaginable, reds, greens, golds, blues, purples, silvers. They were accompanied by miniature wooden figures of Father Christmas, reindeer, gnomes, hearts, and stars. Pine cones dusted in silver and gold lay in glass bowls. Everything sparkled and scintillated, whilst the hum of conversation surrounded her, as people touched and discussed the magical items waiting to be brought to life on a Christmas tree. She glanced from side to side, not knowing quite where to look first. Someone wound up the key of a snow dome lying close to her in amongst other snow globes and brightly-painted, musical boxes. A tune started to tinkle from it, she struggled to listen above the other sounds in the shop. What was that melody? She just couldn't remember what it was called as it carved out its brittle notes from between the buzz of low, excited voices. She stared at the globe, the artificial snow still swirled under the glass dome, and she tried to make out what else was inside it as she peered closely. The snow settled upon a glittering, silver palace, there were two deer standing by the entrance and a tree, all in white. With a start of surprise she realised that upon the branches of the tree hung the tiniest of blue fir cones.

'Would you like that Katy?' Grandpa Ron asked. Katy nodded slowly.

'It looks like the pine tree you have in the garden, I think it is lovely.' She picked the globe up carefully, the tinkling music had stopped, but a few dustings of snow fell from the turrets of the palace landing on the deer. She held it tightly in her hand until they ended up at the till, as they had a little more shopping to do. Grandma Rose had told them to buy some new lights for the Christmas tree and Katy chose a beautifully adorned bell as a present for Ruthie. She was pleased to hear the bell jangled quite loudly when she shook it from side to side, it had dancers carved into it which she knew Ruthie would love.

They went into the café where Katy had a drink of hot chocolate with cinnamon sprinkles and Grandpa Ron had a very strong cup of tea, they both had crumpets with butter oozing out of them and dripping onto their plates. The café was warm and full of delicious smells, laughter and chatting. Not for the first time Katy wished her sister was with her to enjoy it too.

When they returned home Grandma Rose was pleased to hear that the Christmas tree would be arriving so quickly. She was sat at the kitchen table writing cards which she soon afterwards sent Katy to deliver to the post box at the end of their road. Katy had to pass the new house next door, the gravel drive led up to a grand entrance and outside was parked a silver sports car. The house had enormous windows and at one of them she could see a shadow of someone looking out onto the road. That must be Mr Entwhistle, she thought to herself. She didn't know much about him and hadn't met him. Every time she had come down on holiday to Torquay his house had been at various stages of construction whilst he had been abroad. She ran to the post box and squeezed the cards into it. There was a soft mizzle beginning as she walked back to her grandparents' home, its moisture drifting across the landscape like a fragile veil. Over the distant moors she could see the darkened clouds roll in across the granite tors. The misty teardrops clung to her eyelashes and adorned her coat. She had forgotten about Mr Entwhistle, but he still watched her as she turned back into the gate next door.

Humphrey Entwhistle was not a nice man, he used to be a traffic warden. However he had used an inheritance from a distant relative to travel the world and dabble in recreating himself as a famous explorer and zoologist specialising in insects. Another stroke of luck had come, when on a trip to Sumatra to study armoured spiders, he had inadvertently found a hitherto unknown leech stuck to his ear on his return to England. Ignoring the fact this meant he had not given his ears a good clean for two weeks before arriving home, the papers went wild about his new discovery. The Royal National Zoological Society demanded he give a lecture on the jungles of Sumatra, his dangerous exploration and masterful capture of Hirudo Humphrey (hirudo being Latin for leech), which Humphrey was only too happy to do once he had employed a ghost writer to make it all up for him.

Humphrey lived next door to Katy's grandparents. His inheritance meant he had been able to knock down the old house which had existed beforehand and build an ultra-modern home for himself. Everything was fully automated, which meant he didn't have to do much except press a few buttons, to cook a roast dinner, make his bed and give himself a haircut practically all at the same time. Unfortunately he still didn't feel the creation of steel and glass he called home was big enough, and had hit on the idea of persuading Katy's grandparents to move, so that he could buy their house and build a museum dedicated to himself. Much to his annoyance they very politely refused, so he had made an opening in his fence and erected a special badger run, which meant the creatures disappeared into Grandpa Ron's garden every night to dig up flower bulbs, and create potholes in his lawn.

Humphrey often stared at night through his very expensive binoculars to watch the destruction next door, rubbing his hands in glee whilst muttering to himself, 'It can't be long now!' Entwhistle was counting on wearing down the elderly couple through various underhand methods.

He had invested in a great deal of Japanese knotweed (very nasty stuff, do not grow it in your garden whatever you do) which he intended to plant in secret next door, until a lady from the council, Miss Bussell, had wind of it and demanded he get rid of it. He also lit bonfires of his old socks at regular intervals until the whole road complained, which they might not have done if he had washed them first. The same lady from the council came around wearing a scarf over her mouth asking him to fill out a special form, after which she sent council workers to fumigate his garden.

No, Humphrey Entwhistle was not nice at all, but he

was a celebrity and had made an important discovery, apparently, so allowances were made in many quarters, but luckily not by Miss Bussell. The press and media weren't to know Hirudo Humphrey had been found by accident. Humphrey felt he had more than earned his fame by the fact he had painfully extracted the leech and noticed it was an unusual orange colour with purple stripes. Everything else had just fallen into place. With this fame had come more money, he had formed Entwhistle Enterprises and was looking to close an old people's home on the other side of town called "Whispering Pines" so that he could turn it into luxury flats.

He thought he had seen Katy before, getting on to the train where he'd had an unfortunate encounter with a red lollipop and an uncivilised toddler. She would probably turn out to be related to those nuisance Clutterbucks no doubt. He turned from the window and snorted in an irritable way, if only he could get them to move. He was desperate to get his hands on their house. He picked up the local newspaper lying on his kitchen table.

'Ah this is better,' he thought to himself as he gazed at his own photograph showing him shaking hands with the town's mayoress. It was a piece on the front page talking about all his exploits and the fact he was going to be at the shop "Print-a-Porter" signing copies of his recent book.

He sighed with contentment, and looked around his home, this was the life! He was especially proud of his portrait hanging over his bed. It had been painted by an up and coming artist who, he just knew, would be famous in a few years' time and the portrait would then be worth a lot of money. The fact the portrait showed him with a square head and protuberant triangular eyes did not dissuade him from this theory. There also appeared to be a particularly fearsome creature staring out from the background, which most onlookers assumed to be Hirudo Humphrey. The leech did not appear to be very happy about having been discovered in the jungles of Sumatra, and looked as if it would have much preferred to be un-discovered again, whereas Humphrey Entwhistle on the other hand would be totally happy, or so he thought, if he could just get his hands on the Clutterbucks' house.

Meanwhile, totally unaware of the ill-wishing celeb-rity next door, Rose Clutterbuck was getting into her car with Katy. They were going to do some Christmas shopping in the town centre, mainly for Grandpa Ron's present, but also for Christmas crackers she had forgotten to buy. The town was bustling with life and colour and as there were not so many shopping days until December the 25th people were rushing to do their last minute gift hunting. Christmas lights strung across the street began to glitter and glow in the late afternoon dusk. The shop windows were warm and inviting. Grandma Rose could not decide between two jumpers she had spotted last week for her husband, but eventually Katy persuaded her to take the one with snowflakes on it rather than the one with a reindeer sporting a rather large red nose. She couldn't imagine Grandpa Ron would wear Rudolph to keep himself warm more than one day a year! The jostling crowds outside the shop seemed to be full of people Grandma Rose knew and it took a long time to reach the car as she kept stopping for a chat and a "Merry Christmas!" As they eventually approached the house with all their parcels they saw Freddie outside the front door.

'Come in, come in!' Grandma Rose handed him some of her parcels. 'I'm sure you'll have some tea with us while you chat to Katy. Does your mum know you're here?'

Freddie's mum worked as a doctor in the local hospital, which was very busy at the moment with flu patients due to the time of year. There also seemed to be a lot of Christmas babies arriving.

'Oh yes it's fine. Amy is at her friend's house today for tea, mum says she'll pick her up on the way home from work.'

Amy was Freddie's younger sister, she loved dinosaurs, super heroes, football and marshmallows, but only the pink ones. She was a fierce little ball of energy, never sitting still and chatting nineteen to the dozen from one end of the day to the next. Her favourite words were "why" and "no" and she sprinkled all her conversations with them like hundreds and thousands on a fairy cake.

Freddie spotted Katy's snow globe on the mantelpiece above the Clutterbucks' very old fireplace.

'Hey what's that?' He took it down very carefully, twisting it in his hand to make the tiny snowflakes dance and twirl around the little figures inside which were reflected in the lenses of his glasses. He gazed entranced

33

at the miniature world encapsulated beneath the semi-sphere. Katy smiled at him before saying in a mysterious voice, 'Come into the garden.' She led the way outside down the path lit by solar lights, past the log pile, past the winter-flowering clematis, past the wine-coloured helle-bores and stopped in front of the pine tree adorned with lavender-blue pine cones.

'Look at that.'

Freddie looked at the snow-globe and looked back at the pine tree. 'Why they're the same!'

'Yes, that's what I thought. Grandpa says it comes from somewhere really, really cold, he did mention it might be somewhere in Russia, but he's not sure, he's lost the label. I found the caterpillar on it the other day, you know, the one in the jar.'

'Oh yes your mystery pet, the one I couldn't see, why don't we take a look now?'

'Well I don't think you'll see much, it's turned into a chrysalis, - or I think it's a chrysalis. To tell you the truth I'm not really sure.' She frowned at him.

'Let's investigate,' Freddie answered. But just then

Grandma Rose called them in for tea. Sausage rolls, cheese sandwiches and chocolate cake kept them occupied for a while until the children felt stuffed with food. Afterwards they played monopoly and Grandpa Ron won as usual. Grandma Rose kept ending up in jail for some strange reason, and Katy soon ran out of money, but before Freddie left, the children went upstairs to check on the caterpillar.

The jar was on the dressing table. Katy lifted it up to the light, but the chrysalis was nowhere to be seen.

'Let me look Kat,' Freddie took the jar from Katy's hand and untwisted the lid gently until it was completely unscrewed. He lifted the lid slowly and started to poke around in the leaves and twigs.

'I don't think there is anything in here Katy.'

'But it can't have gone, how could it get out?'

Then very slowly Freddie turned the lid over in his hand. Stood on it was something looking like a moth or a butterfly, but it was unlike any moth or butterfly either of them had ever seen before. It shimmered with a blue-white light, it had one pair of wings and the head was clearly distinct from the body. It started to rise up with flapping wings towards the window, and as it did so Katy noticed something dart from its mouth, it looked like a pale flame which lit the pane for a moment then went out. On the glass it had left tiny little crystals, or so it looked to Katy and Freddie. Freddie whistled softly in amazement.

'What have you found Kat?' He pointed to it. 'I've never seen an insect like that before. Where did you say your grandpa bought the tree? I bet there's nothing else like it in this country, who knows where it could have come from?' He suddenly looked thoughtful, 'I guess an expert might be able to tell you. I've got a great idea, your next door neighbour is having a book signing session tomorrow afternoon, I could meet you after school and we could go down together and find out what it is. He should be able to help, after all he knows about stuff like that.'

'You mean ask Mr Entwhistle? I thought you didn't like him?'

'Well to be fair I don't really know him, it's just that he's trying to buy the home where my grandad lives, Whispering Pines and they're all very worried about it.'

'Ok, perhaps, let me think about it Freddie.'

Freddie grinned, 'Of course we will have to catch it first and put it back into the jar.'

'No, leave it for now, there's a net for clearing the pond in the conservatory, I can catch it later. Let it fly around for a bit.'

'I'd better go, homework to do. Would you believe it! Nearly the holidays and we still get homework! See you tomorrow!'

Katy walked to the bottom of the driveway with Freddie. He lived just across the road from Katy's grandparents, a little further down on the right. His mum was just arriving back from picking up Amy and when they spotted Katy they both waved at her. Amy had her hair in bunches as usual (she wouldn't have it any other way!) and was wearing a Spiderman T-shirt. Katy smiled at them and waved back. She slowly climbed the stairs to her room inching the door open so as not to let the creature onto the landing. It was flittering against the glass pane which looked out into the garden. Katy thought for a moment.

'Will you be alright?' Katy asked it quietly as she opened the window to let it fly away. A large moon, almost full, peered down at them. It bathed the garden in a soft, silvery light making everything mysterious and unknown. Beyond it twinkled the winter stars making their own music millions of miles away, just like her snow globe.

'Goodbye,' Katy whispered as it flew over the sill and out into the indigo night. She shut the window with a sigh and went to bed.

HUMPHREY
ENTWHISTLE

T he next morning the Christmas tree was delivered. The lorry which backed into their
driveway narrowly missed the gate posts,
but the men who drove it were kind enough to carry the
tree inside. After much huffing and puffing, they stuck it
into the tree stand that Katy's grandparents always used.
They spent twenty minutes making sure it was straight
before they left, with a twenty pound note they'd reluc-

tantly accepted from Grandpa Ron.

'She's a beauty alright.' Grandma Rose was delighted with the tree once they had cut the netting which encased it. The boughs unfurled gracefully, their perfume filled the whole house and with it came the expectation of Christmas. Up in the attic Grandpa Ron sorted out all the decorations, passing the boxes to Katy standing by the steps. They started to unpack them by the tree, Grandma Rose brought in a tray of hot chocolate drinks and as she did so she glanced up at the topmost branch.

'I thought you were going to put the lights on first,' she said to her husband.

'Of course,' he answered slightly surprised. Putting the tray down Grandma Rose pointed to the tree's green spire

'Well what's that? You've put a fairy on it. Did you buy it at the Christmas tree farm?'

Grandpa Ron frowned, 'No, what are you'm talking about?'

He stood back and looked up at the tree. Katy gasped, for there sitting on the top was the gauzy-winged insect she had let out of her bedroom window the night before.

It looked a little larger than Katy remembered from last night and did indeed have a resemblance to a very small, dainty Christmas fairy.

'Oh I think it is my caterpillar.'

Both Katy's grandparents stared at her and then stared at the top of the tree again.

'But that's not a caterpillar.'

'No, but you see it hatched yesterday.'

'Hatched?'

'Yes and I let it out of the window, but it seems to have come back. I'll get the pond net and catch it.'

Katy's grandparents looked at her a little bemused. Luckily the net had a very long handle so she only had to stand a few steps up on the ladder to catch the little creature, which she then quickly deposited back into the large jar upstairs in her bedroom. It crawled around the glass of the jar, its wings twitching. Katy looked at it carefully. She realised it only had four legs, but insects normally have six she thought to herself. Now and then it looked as if a ghostly tongue flickered in and out of its mouth leaving small deposits on the glass. She pulled a book out of the bookcase in the hallway on insects. She had seen some unusual things in her grandparents' home and garden, especially in the summertime. Once Ruthie had run screaming from the sitting room into the kitchen because a horntail wasp, with what looked like an enormous sting, had buzzed into it. However it was harmless, the 'sting' only used to burrow into pine wood to lay eggs. She had also spotted a humming bird moth once hovering over some water lilies in the pond, hanging in the air as it drew nectar from the flowers. They'd had to put netting over the pond eventually as a heron appeared one year trying to steal fish from it. Year after year tiny baby frogs had hatched in the garden, hopping along the path so the children would tiptoe along it, scooping them up and putting them somewhere safe. Grandpa had even found a fully grown one hiding inside the reel of the hose pipe once, staring up at him with hooded eyes.

She flicked through the section on British insects, but there was nothing resembling what was in her jar. All the butterflies and moths she could find had two sets of wings, her little creature only had one and it had come back to her despite her setting it free last night. Katy was becoming more intrigued, especially as she realised it had grown visibly bigger in the space of one day. Soon the jar would be far too small if it carried on at this rate, it seemed that if she wanted to know what it was Freddie had the best idea. She would meet him after school as he'd suggested and they would ask Mr Entwhistle. It couldn't do any harm could it?

Later that day the town was still very busy with Christmas shoppers. A huge tree stood in the town centre festooned with twinkling lights and people laden down with bags and parcels were laughing and smiling as they passed one another in the street.

Humphrey was sat inside the local bookshop which was decorated with great swathes of red and green artificial holly, ready to entertain his fans waiting to buy his latest book. As a publicity stunt the shop had suggested that anyone who came to buy a signed copy of his book was invited to bring their pet along to be shown to him. A lady in a large, fluffy, purple cardigan who happened to be the manageress of the shop "Print-a-Porter" had brought him a cup of coffee and two chocolate biscuits, which she set down at his desk behind an enormous pile of his books. The title stared up at him: "The Endeavours of Entwhistle in South Africa". It was accompanied by a photograph of him in a pith helmet, with a pair of binoculars around his neck. His shorts displayed his rather knobbly knees and legs with ginger hairs, there was a rain frog looking up at him adoringly, balanced on his hand. They looked like twins, frog and man, with their short stumpy legs and goggling eyes.

A small queue had formed in an orderly manner in front of the desk waiting patiently as he slurped his coffee and wiped crumbs from his shirt. A little old lady wearing a red beret and flowery wellingtons shuffled up with her shopping baggage and propped it up against a leg of the desk as she produced a tortoiseshell cat from a cage in a shopping trolley. It was raining outside and she had wanted to keep Daisy dry.

'Say hello to the nice man Daisy.' The old lady stroked Daisy, murmuring lovingly into her feline ear, whilst holding her up for Humphrey's approval.

Humphrey sighed heavily. He got a gold pen from the

desk and opened the cover of one of his books.

'What would you like me to write?' he asked inquiringly.

'Oh um, "To my Daisy Waisy, pusskins please." The author looked a little nonplussed.

'Er, certainly Daisy Waisy.' Humphrey flourished the pen expertly and started to write.

'NO!' The little lady started to laugh, 'I'm not Daisy.' She buried her head into the cat's face, 'This is Daisy.'

'I see, um - does your cat read?' He said as an attempt at a joke.

'No silly, I thought you were a zoologist. She purrs, don't you Daisy?'

The cat obligingly started up like an engine dribbling all over the page Humphrey was writing on. The ink slowly dissolved on his signature, Humphrey liked to write in fountain pen as it seemed more in keeping with his literary standing than a biro. He handed the book to the little old lady.

'Oh my you're not giving me that one are you?'

'Why not?'

'Well it's wet isn't it. I mean I am expected to pay for it aren't I?'

'Perhaps we can come to some compromise,' Humphrey put on his most oily, persuasive voice. 'After all it was your cat who made it wet. Shall we say ten per cent off?' Daisy and her owner scowled at him.

'Well, here's me on a tiny pension, spent my bus fare getting down here and now you want to charge me for damaged goods.' Her pink fingers starting tapping on the desk top.

The rest of the book-signing queue were starting to get interested in their conversation now and looked restless.

Humphrey bridled, he was darned if his, (well not really his), hard work was going to go unpaid.

Humphrey had failed to notice a certain streetwise expression on the elderly lady's face. Her soft Devonshire accents had cloaked a native shrewdness that bespoke ill of anyone attempting to thwart her Machiavellian designs.

'Oh well,' Humphrey stopped himself from reverting to traffic warden mode. 'Of course you must have this book free.' He attempted a friendly smile through gritted teeth, large and white, looking more like those of a crocodile floating on the Zambezi River than an affable author and explorer.

'Thank you, thank you,' twittered the cat owner as she grabbed the book and stuffed it in the shopping trolley with Daisy.

Humphrey looked further down the line of people waiting to see him. They had with them an assortment of cages, pets on leads, glass tanks and someone had even hauled a crate in on a trolley which looked rather large. Goodness knows what was in that.

Humphrey had realised very early on in his celebrity career that unfortunately he didn't really like animals that much at all. However early success had given something to cash in on and he wasn't about to give it up now. The fact was during his "expeditions" he found the most luxurious hotels to sit in, whilst paying someone to do his exploring and animal discovering for him. And if anyone tried to take a photograph of him sat by the swimming pool sipping a horribly garish cocktail, their phone either ended up in the pool or the cocktail landed on their head.

He suddenly noticed a familiar face in the waiting throng, wasn't that the girl who had come to stay with the Clutterbucks next door? He had seen her twice now, on the train when he'd returned after promoting his new book in London and walking down to the post box outside his house.

'Good morning!' A boy of around ten plonked a bird-cage containing a rose-feathered cockatoo next to the books on the desk.

'I've come to show you my bird.' He grinned widely, showing a bright green tongue which had recently enjoyed the benefit of a gob-stopper.

Feeling he was on firmer ground now Humphrey pulled the cage towards him.

'YOW!!' Humphrey jumped out of his chair and furiously sucked his thumb. The cockatoo had casually taken a chunk out of it through the bars. Obviously feeling pleased with itself it chuckled and said, 'Pieces of eight, pieces of eight.'

Humphrey had knocked the coffee flying across the shop, and now the cockatoo strained to reach one of the nibbled chocolate biscuits lying next to its cage. With a triumphant squawk the bird grabbed it in its bill and pulled it in through the bars. The shop manager in the fluffy, purple cardigan came over bringing a mop with her, tut tutting, and muttering about health and safety.

The boy bent double with laughter, tears began to trickle from the corners of his eyes as he gasped with hysteria. Eventually he stopped laughing enough to get some words out.

'Long John always likes his snacks, sorry.' He guffawed once again. 'Sorry, sorry. Mum and I wondered if you could take a look at him, Long John that is, 'cos she thinks he may have worms.'

Humphrey recoiled hastily, as Long John offered him the last of the chocolate biscuit through the birdcage, as compensation for a nipped digit.

'Look here young man I am not a vet, I am an author, I cannot cure your pet's worms. I am sorry but there it is.'

Some of the members of the book-signing queue, alerted by this information, picked up their pets and headed for the shop exit.

'Now what would you like me to write in your copy of my book?'

'Eh?' The boy hopped from one foot to the other. 'Errr?' He said in an attempt to sound more intelligent as Humphrey looked at him expectantly.

'What book?' He nervously juggled the remaining gobstoppers in his pocket, whilst surreptitiously reaching for Long John's cage. He'd seen the sign outside the bookshop about advice for pets, but failed to realise he'd be expected to purchase a book.

'This is a book signing, young man, are you here under false pretences?' Long John's owner had watched enough police serials to know he could well be on sticky ground and not entirely due to gob-stoppers. Looking at the cockatoo for inspiration his face brightened.

'Oh dear, Long John's face looks a bit swollen, I think he might of caught the mumps off my brother. So sorry, I didn't realise it could still be affectious.' With that, impressed by his own quick thinking, he grabbed the bird-cage and took the wormy, mumptious cockatoo back to the sweetshop for a second helping of gobstoppers.

Humphrey was beginning to feel that perhaps this particular book signing gimmick was not such a good idea. He had given one book away and lost the use of a thumb.

It was with some trepidation Humphrey watched a teenager in a leather biker jacket approach him holding a glass tank, he had a nasty premonition that this could hold his nemesis. In amongst some leaves and twigs a pair of eyes gleamed at him, unblinkingly.

'Alright mate?' The teenager sniffed loudly. 'I love your documentaries.'

Humphrey frowned, he hadn't made any to his knowledge, he had only "done" chat shows, but wasn't going to enlighten his prospective book customer.

'Er yes, thank you and who do we have here?'

'Well it's Nigel init.'

'Ahhh!' The snake had a yellow and black collar and small regular black markings down its side, over a metre

long, it was lying in a languid coil and stared at him inso-
lently.

'I can take him out if you like, want to hold him?'

Humphrey tried to restrain the expression of fear which threatened to flicker across his face. He could stick anything in the animal kingdom if he had to - but not snakes.

'That is kind of you but probably not.' The snake and its owner looked a little crestfallen, but both brightened at Humphrey's next words.

'He is a fine specimen however of Natrix Helvetica. You obviously take great care of him.' The snake looked suitably modest although still pinning Humphrey with its eyes which seemed to be rotating in ever smaller circles the longer he looked into them. It was with some effort that he fixed his own stare onto the face of the teenager, which itself seemed to be rotating as the young man chewed a stick of gum.

'And who shall I dedicate the book to?'

'Ahh yes, me mum, she loves you too.'

'And what is her name?'

'Judith.' Humphrey's pen slid quickly across the page

and he handed the book back to its new owner, hoping against hope he wouldn't bother to read the inscription before he had paid and was out of the shop.

'Ta mate.'

The teenager removed himself and it was to Humphrey's relief that Katy appeared from behind him in the queue, holding a very large, pickled onion jar containing blue pine cones and sprigs of holly.

Katy cleared her throat and popped the jar upon the desk.

'Excuse me, I expect you've seen lots of really wild creatures on your travels and I don't want to waste your time, but have you ever seen anything like this before?'

She turned the jar around so that Humphrey could look into it. At first he could only see the cones and the holly, but then his eyes still reeling from the hypnotic effects of the snake began to focus more clearly.

There nestled in the holly berries were a pair of iridescent wings, they shimmered a pearly white, but as the light caught them the wings exploded in a kaleidoscope of colour. Humphrey watched in awe as the wings slowly began to beat, not as those of a butterfly or moth, but more like a bird as it takes to the air. But strangest of all, the head of the creature was almost like that of a tiny dinosaur. He watched fascinated as the insect or whatever it might be, flew to the top of the jar where the lid stopped it getting free. It crawled around for a few seconds, then suddenly the glass of the jar became strangely patterned where it sat, like frost in winter upon a window pane.

'Do you know what it is?' Katy asked him. She was conscious of Freddie waiting for her patiently by the book shop entrance.

Humphrey swallowed hard, he had never seen anything like it in all his travels.

'Well I am not sure, but if you would like to leave the jar with me I can study it and let you know what I find out.' His voice was husky with barely contained excitement and he went to grab the jar from the desk, but she was quicker. With a quick swoop, the jar was in her hands.

'Oh I just thought you might know something right away.' She turned to go and as she did so Humphrey said,

'I know you don't I? You're staying with Mr and Mrs Clutterbuck next door to me. I can pop round one day if you like and let you know if I discover anything. Or I can take the jar now if you will let me.' He made it sound like an order, or was it more of a threat?

'Thank you, sorry but I have to meet my friend.' She made her way through the throngs of shoppers to Freddie.

'Any good?' he asked her. She shook her head and pushed the heavy shop door open, putting the jar into Grandma Rose's basket.

'I sort of wish I hadn't shown it to him now, you should have seen his face, he looked as if he might gobble it up.' Katy shivered, 'I think you're right, he isn't a very nice man.'

Meanwhile Humphrey sat behind his pile of books totally oblivious to the fact Katy had left without buying one. He might not have discovered much himself (except by accident), but he'd seen the results of what he'd paid others to do. Not once had he seen anything quite like what he'd seen in that pickle jar. Was it an insect? Was it a weird bird? That was the trouble with fame, once you had a taste for it you had to carry on discovering things to keep it. He was hoping to get an honorary professorship from a local university soon, but his last trip to Eastern Europe and Mongolia had been a little disappointing for him, despite an almost lethal encounter with an Amur tiger when he'd been at a Siberian zoo.

He sat ruminating about how to get his hands on the jar Katy had brought in for a better look, what if it was yet another new find, a new revelation like Hirudo Humphrey? He was suddenly brought back down to earth by a loud cough, an angelic looking child stood in front of him holding something behind her back.

'Hello,' she lisped through a gap in her upper front teeth. Her mother stood next to her gazing upon her lovingly.

'Can I thow you my stick inthect? And mummy wants to buy your book.'

This was more like it, thought Humphrey.

'Of course my dear,' he answered, sounding like a cross between Father Christmas and the big bad wolf in Little

Red Riding Hood.

'If thoo look closthly thoo can see her.' The child produced a well ventilated container containing potting earth and some leaves. The sides had slight condensation on them.

Humphrey turned the container this way and that, but he couldn't seem to see anything.

'I'm afraid I can't see any stick insects in here.'

The mother looked at him slightly disapprovingly.

'Of course you can.' She said. 'Please can I have one of your books, I would like it dedicated to my gran, she's a great fan of yours.'

'And what is gran's name?'

The angelic apparition chimed in, 'It'sth Thelithity.'

'Oh that's unusual,' Humphrey felt pretty confident he'd put in enough t's and h's as he put pen to paper.

'Now can thoo thee the inthect?' She put her face up against the container and after a short interval started to wail.

'She's gone mummy.'

'What?' The child's mother stared through the plastic and pulled her mobile phone out of her pocket, pressing buttons with the speed of light.

'Bartholomew, Bartholomew where's that stick insect now? What do you mean you took it for a walk? Get Daddy on the phone, get him right now. .... Jeremy, Jeremy, find that insect immediately. I do not want to find it in the chocolate-finger biscuit tin again. What do you mean Bartholomew's been cleaning the dog's ears out with it?!'

She threw the phone into her handbag, 'Men!' And then grabbed the book from off the desk with the background music of her sobbing child. 'What's this?' she said as she thrust the open book under Humphrey's nose. He was quite unused to being on the receiving end of such force-fulness, he was usually dishing it out.

'With all best wishes to Thelithity, yours truly Humphrey Entwhistle.' he replied faithfully reading it out.

'What does that mean?'

'Well what it says,' he definitely felt the lack of a more

adequate retort.

'Felicity, her name is Felicity,' and with that throwing the book back on to the table and sweeping her weeping child into her arms, she turned on her heel and left the shop.

It was a shame, thought Humphrey, that Thelithity was such an unusual name. Yet another wasted book. When a day went badly, it went badly and there was nothing you could do about it. However, that Clutterbuck girl might have brought something really unusual in, so it might not have been such an awful day after all. If only he could get his hands on it for a closer look.

I t was very unfortunate for Humphrey Entwhistle that the next morning news was heard announcing Professor von Flusspferd, missing for two years, had in fact been found safe and well. He had been rescued from the depths of the Amazon jungle in a bi-plane mapping an area which, up until now, had been little explored.

Of course Humphrey at that point had no idea that this was unfortunate for him and began the morning reading his bank balance, which always cheered him up, along with his usual breakfast of two poached eggs on toast. It wasn't until he switched on his super screen TV hanging on the kitchen wall that he saw Professor von Flusspferd appear. Despite wearing what seemed to be a huge bush on his head and a very long straggly beard the professor seemed to be the picture of health. He had a big smile on his face and his eyes twinkled with good humour. However he could also be very unpredictable in his moods, as one of his interviewers was about to find out.

'Professor, I expect you are glad to be coming home? I believe you have made quite a number of discoveries during the two years you have been lost in the Amazon?'

'Yes of course, I haf found many, many things that vill be off great importance!' The Professor beamed. 'It is of course zo lucky zat my notebooks and camera haf been rescued also.'

'Yes of course you will be happy to meet up with fellow zoologists to discuss your findings, people like Lord Jaspar Finkbottom and Humphrey Entwhistle.'

'Vot!' exploded the professor, 'Zat imposter?! He is an idiot of zee first degree. He could not find his vay out off zee papiertutte.'

The reporter displayed some embarrassment. 'Well he is a peer of the realm Professor, I don't think we should call him an idiot. He has made some astounding discoveries which he has shared with the world.'

'Nein dummkopf! Not Finkbottom, Entvhistle, Entvhistle.' At this point Professor Flusspferd glared and pointed threateningly at the camera. 'I vill expose you Entvistle! I haf proof zat you are not vot you claim!'

The reporter had taken a step back at this as the professor had looked quite fierce, but he was also secretly looking forward to the promise of a lot of lively interviews to come.

Humphrey Entwhistle sat frozen at his kitchen table staring at the TV screen, with a mouth full of toast which he had forgotten to chew threatening to choke him. Professor von Flusspferd's eyes bored into Humphrey's.

What could the professor know? Humphrey tried to

think back over the past few years since becoming famous, for two of them Professor von Flusspferd had been lost in the jungles of the Amazon. What could he possibly know?? And then it became clear as the reporter turned to someone stood next to the Professor.

'Marjory Farthing, we are of course very happy to welcome you back from the jungle too, anything you would like to say to the world?'

A lady with dark beetle eyebrows glowered at the camera forcing an insincere grimace masquerading as a smile. 'Of course, we are very pleased to have the opportunity of studying everything we have found with the rest of the scientific community. And with some of its members in particular.' Her lips parted to reveal protruding teeth and a snake-like tongue darting between them.

Humphrey gasped in horror, Marjory alive? But the last time he had seen her she had been drifting in a balloon over the Sumatran jungle looking for leaf monkeys. The fact he had forgotten to report her missing had entirely slipped his mind. How had she survived? What was she doing with Professor von Flusspferd? And most importantly did she still expect him to marry her?

A whole jumble of questions threatened to overwhelm his overtaxed brain. His eyes were getting bloodshot with the effort and he was spluttering toast at the television screen. Suddenly the foundations on which he had built a lucrative career threatened to bring his whole life tumbling down. Something would have to be done and then he remembered Katy and the strange little creature in the jar. It had been like nothing he had seen before, of course he wasn't to know how much stranger the creature would become in the next few days. But one thing he did know was that he had to get his hands on it, to find out if it really was as unusual as he thought it might be. It might save him still!

That same morning had a very different beginning for Katy. The sun streamed in through her bedroom window. It lit up the dust motes dancing across the room, sparkling like beings from another world.

Katy's eyes felt very heavy, with a struggle she opened them and looked around. Where was the creature? She remembered that she had not put it back into the jar again, its wings had sprouted so much by the time Katy came up to sleep the previous night, that the poor thing had floundered to stand upright inside its glass prison. It had also seemed to have grown what looked like a very long, narrow tail. No, that can't be right, she had thought to herself. She felt very confused as this strange little thing was certainly no insect that was certain, but in that case what was it?

Katy had opened her window in the evening trying to usher it through, hoping it would take the opportunity to escape, but no. At first it got tangled in the curtains, its tail thrashing uselessly until Katy rescued it from them, then it flew straight back inside, landing on top of the wardrobe behind a shoe box. Katy didn't want to frighten it, so she left it there when she went to bed. Whilst she had waited to go to sleep she had stared at the carvings on her wardrobe, her drooping eyes seemed to see the mice scampering in and out of the bluebells where they were joined by wee, little, silver butterflies flitting hither and thither. The last thing she had been aware of was a strange fluttering coming from the top of the wardrobe before she'd drifted into a deep, uninterrupted sleep.

Now she became aware of a pair of very bright green eyes staring at her over the top of the shoe box. The creature waddled out from behind its hiding place. Katy's jaw dropped, for there, without a doubt, sat a small dragon. How had it grown so much in such a short time? It was the size of a squirrel. She could see the newly sprouted tail waving from side to side as it surveyed her through its unblinking gaze. Katy's heart began to thump wildly, whether in excitement or nervousness she couldn't tell. She'd been bitten by a dog when she was younger and she certainly didn't fancy being bitten by a dragon. And hang on! Didn't dragons breathe fire? The thought produced a sensation of foreboding in the pit of her stomach and she was just deciding whether to run from the bedroom when the dragon made an extraordinary noise. It sounded like a cross between tearing tissue paper and a deflating balloon. It shook its burnished, silver-edged, translucent scales which caught the sun streaming through the windows in a blinding flash. Issuing from its mouth came a cold jet of air which settled on Katy's bed frame causing tiny icicles to form. To Katy's astonishment its small nose then twitched and it breathed a warm, gentle puff melting them as quickly as they had been created.

The creature then launched itself from the wardrobe and landed on Katy, licking her face with a very rough tongue. Luckily the dragon had very short, stubby teeth which due to their newness seemed quite clean, Katy wasn't sure she would enjoy being licked by a fully grown dragon which hadn't used a toothbrush and had eaten ....er, yes that was a point, what was the dragon going to eat? Up until now that hadn't really been a problem, but what did a juvenile dragon enjoy for breakfast? Katy realised she would have to get ready without delay to stop her grandmother knocking on the door and popping her head around it to see what she wanted on her toast this morning.

Katy hurriedly got dressed and after gently putting the dragon inside her wardrobe she went down into the kitchen to see what she could find to feed it with.

She opened the cupboard door above the bread bin, it

was full of jars. She liked marmite on her toast, but she knew Ruthie hated it, what if the dragon didn't like it? In the end she settled on strawberry jam, as most people like that she thought to herself. She put two slices of bread into the toaster and as she did so she glanced out into the garden. The holly bush was thick with berries, which several birds pecked at hungrily. Oh dear – she suddenly realised, perhaps she should be looking for something out in the garden for it to eat, like seeds in the blue pine cones?

Just as she was pondering over this the toast popped into the air and at the same time there was a shriek from upstairs. It seemed to be coming from her bedroom. Her grandparents' cat Mouser looked up from his basket where he had been dozing peacefully next to the oven. Katy dashed from the kitchen and met her grandpa coming in from the garden.

'What on earth is going on?' he said to her in a worried voice.

Katy didn't answer, she rushed past him, her heart thudding in time to her footsteps running up the stairs. When she opened the bedroom door she saw Grandma

Rose sat on the floor in front of the wardrobe and in her lap was the dragon looking very smug with a sock in its mouth. Katy was aware of her grandpa arriving behind her at the door.

'Where did that come from?' Grandpa Ron pointed at the dragon, he was having trouble fully understanding the scene before him. 'It can't stay in your bedroom! Whatever next! Let's help your grandma get on to the bed.'

He tentatively lifted the dragon up first, putting it on the pile of laundry that Grandma Rose had been collecting to wash that morning. It had been left strewn about the floor next to the wardrobe she had been opening when she had been surprised by their extraordinary visitor jumping out of it. The wee dragon squeaked in protest, quite difficult with a mouth full of sock, swinging its tail in disgust as Grandpa Ron deposited it on the hillock of clothes.

'Dear, dear, you can't go giving your gran frights like this at her time of life!' Ron said to Katy shaking his head as they helped Rose onto Katy's duvet.

'Oi! I'm not as old as all that Ron Clutterbuck!' replied Katy's grandma sitting on the bed. 'Just gave me a shock that's all. But where in the world has this latest animal of yours come from Katy? And more to the point what is it??'

The dragon's green eyes followed Katy as she plonked herself on the bed next to her grandmother. It dropped the sock and looked at her quizzically as if to say: 'I'd like to know that too!'

'Well,' began Katy slowly, 'You remember the caterpillar I found on Grandpa's blue pine tree that turned into the Christmas fairy?'

'Yes,' chorused her grandparents.

'Er, well it's grown a bit!'

Her grandparents looked at Katy in disbelief. Then they stared at the remarkable creature snuffling amongst the laundry. The dragon shook itself and its scales tinkled softly, throwing reflected sunlight on to the bedroom walls.

'You mean that there beast has grown over a few days out of that tiny worm?' Her grandma gasped. 'How big is it going to get?'

Katy shrugged apologetically. 'I don't know,' she replied. 'I've never had a dragon as a pet before.'

'Well, how's the maid going to answer that Rose? I

don't suppose there's another living being like this one in the whole wide world and I can't see us finding much out on the internet either.' His face brightened. 'But I could check to see if I can remember the name of the tree you found it on, perhaps that could give us a clue?' He brought his phone upstairs and trawled through a gardening website looking at photographs of different pines.

'Well, he said eventually, 'I think the nearest I can get is this one here.' He handed the phone over to Katy. She looked at the screen, it had a name written across it, "Pinus Sibirica – blue smoke". The tree she saw certainly had the feathery needles and lavender cones like the pine in the garden, but it wasn't quite the same, as the cones on the tree in their garden were edged with silver. They looked somehow more magical than these pictures she decided.

'Come to think of it,' said Grandpa Ron frowning, 'I'm not sure that the tree had a label on it when I bought it. I just picked it up at the gardening centre without really noticing. Perhaps it only had a price ticket on it.'

'The fact remains the creature is here now and we

need to decide what we're going to feed it on and where it's going to sleep.' Grandma Rose's practical mind was already going up a gear. 'Then perhaps we could ask Mr Entwhistle next door what it is.

'No!' Katy said vehemently shaking her head, she couldn't help herself. She had taken a strong dislike to the Clutterbucks' neighbour and didn't trust him.

'The zoo then, we could take it to Paignton Zoo and ask them.' Her grandma looked at Katy.

'What do you think?' she asked her.

'Well perhaps we should wait a while, and not make any hasty decisions.' Somehow she didn't feel ready to share her discovery with the world just yet, but she would definitely tell Freddie.

'And I'm going to call it Sybil and it will have to be a she for now, it's easier than calling a dragon 'it' all the time.'

And so it was that the Clutterbucks, a very ordinary family, adopted Sybil a very extraordinary pet.

Ron went into the garden and brought back an assortment of vegetation which he proceeded to wave under

Sybil's nose for her approval as a breakfast dish and settled on some holly berries (bad for humans but good for birds and dragons) and dandelion leaves.

Grandma Rose got an old wash basket out of the garage and put a blanket inside it for Sybil to sleep in, there was room for the dragon to grow too. However Mouser their cat wasn't too impressed when his basket was moved to make room for it by the oven. He eyed Sybil warily as he licked his paws, his tail swishing from side to side as he did so. The one thing in the dragon's favour, as far as Mouser was concerned, was that she didn't seem to like cat food!

Katy thought that it would be important for a growing dragon to have exercise, she was very careful after breakfast to make sure they were not overlooked when she took Sybil into the garden for a run around, but she had not allowed for their next door neighbour and his high magnification binoculars. Katy had already decided that if the dragon decided to leave she wouldn't stop her, so she didn't worry when Sybil suddenly took off and flew into the bay hedge startling two blackbirds and a chattering magpie. Unfortunately the noisy birds drew Humphrey

Entwhistle to his study window. He had been trying to write an intriguing article on the life cycle of Peruvian ants and how they were an acquired delicacy on the menu in South America, in order to settle his nerves after seeing Marjory Farthing back from the dead.

Grandma Rose had duvet covers drying on the washing line, blowing in the sunshine. It was a windy day, dry leaves danced all over the lawn and Mouser galloped after them excitedly trying to pat them with sheathed pads.

What was that? Humphrey squinted at the hedge next door, the birds were making more racket now and he could see something glinting in the winter light. He grabbed his binoculars from the shelf and gazed intently through them. He could just make out .... What was it? If he could just get a little closer. He pulled up the sash window and leant out. It looked like a ..... Well he didn't know what it looked like. It definitely had wings he could tell, but it also shone like no animal he'd seen before unless you counted that strange little thing in the jar the Clutterbuck girl had shown him. Thunderstruck, Humphrey lowered the field glasses. It was the same creature! It was one and the same, but much, much bigger than yesterday!

Meanwhile Sybil was finding the bay leaves were irritating her sensitive dragon nose. She gave an enormous sneeze, the breath from her mouth curled into the air and like a white veil covered the bedding hanging from the washing line from top to bottom. It froze where it hung, rigid and unyielding, like steel. Katy ran up to it and as if knocking at a door, rapped her knuckles on it in amazement. In a moment Sybil was stood next to her on the grass. Having fallen out of the hedge she had stretched her wings and landed gracefully next to the astonished girl. Sybil looked at Katy with her round, emerald eyes, twitched her nose, then very gently sighed, the warmth melting the ice on the duvets and drying them in a trice.

Humphrey Entwhistle watched through the open window, his mouth dropped open, he could not believe what he was seeing. Now more than ever he was determined to get his hands on the strange entity with the shimmering wings.

Katy was completely unaware of any onlooker, but some sixth sense warned Sybil. She glanced towards his house and started to scamper up the garden path towards the kitchen door. Mouser followed, obligingly darting in front of her to use the cat flap allowing them both inside the warm cosy kitchen where they both flopped into their baskets. Katy started to unpeg the washing from the line which was completely dry now and took it into the kitchen. She couldn't understand it, in all the fairy tale books she had read dragons breathed fire, but Sybil quite obviously wasn't a traditional dragon. Was a dragon who breathed ice more dangerous than a dragon who breathed fire? Only time would tell she concluded. Once they had got over their initial shock her grandparents were quick to adapt to the idea of a mythical beast joining the family, but others might not be quite so accepting.

She decided she needed to talk to Freddie as soon as possible, so in the afternoon she met him outside the school gates. His mum had already picked up Amy earlier for her gym club so he was on his own. Katy's grandparents had strict instructions not to let Sybil out as they had noticed a group of reporters gathering outside Humphrey's house next door throughout the day. Freddie was trying to believe what Katy was telling him as they walked home.

'But surely that's impossible!' he exclaimed after hearing Katy's news. He knew the creature was something very unusual, but a dragon?! And one that blew out ice? But then the more he thought about it the more he realised it may be true, the strange frosty patterns on the jar when it had first hatched had to come from something and it was a very odd little animal. Little? From what Katy was telling him it was growing fast.

'And I'm calling it Sybil.'

'Pardon?'

'I'm calling her Sybil,' Katy corrected herself.

'But are you sure it is a girl dragon? Can't we call it Trevor or something?'

'No,' answered Katy, 'she likes being called Sybil.' And indeed the small dragon had seemed to almost purr when Katy had called her name several times that day. Possibly Mouser had been teaching her more than just how to get through the cat flap in the kitchen door.

The children rounded the corner into the road where

they lived and were met by a barrage of cameras and questions.

'Do you live here?' enquired one reporter with a big bushy beard and egg on his tie.

'How long have you known Humphrey Entwhistle?' asked another in a jacket sprinkled with dandruff.

'What do you think about Professor von Flusspferd's comments about him?'

Katy shrank behind Freddie, who took a deep breath to reply to them, as he was quite enjoying the attention, although he hadn't a clue who Professor von Flusspferd was.

'Well ....' he started to say when there was a yell from a lady reporter who had been rummaging inside the wheelie bin stood in Humphrey Entwhistle's driveway. Her legs disappeared from view as she fell in. Her colleagues, torn between getting information from the children and hauling her from the rubbish bin, dithered momentarily before they helped her emerge once more by pulling her out by the ankles.

She laughed triumphantly as she waved what looked

to be a letter in one of her hands, the fact she was covered in potato peelings and a smelly bag which had once contained kippers didn't deter her one bit.

'Ha suckers!!' she exclaimed at the other reporters very unprofessionally.

Katy and Freddie started to edge their way towards the Clutterbucks' house.

'What is it?' the other news teams chorused in unison.

'Looks like a love letter to me,' the untidy and now rather smelly reporter replied waving it in the air. 'Should have shredded it!' The rest all gathered around her, looking over her shoulder.

'Can you make it out what it says with all those baked beans over it?' asked bushy beard.

'Yes, look it's got the word 'love' here,' she pointed to a dark smudge on the paper.

'Hang on,' bushy beard's eyes scanned further down the page which wasn't exactly easy with tomato sauce all over it. 'It says something about Peru and ants.'

The kipper-covered lady looked less sure now. 'Well I'm

certain we can make some sort of story out of it,' she retorted grumpily.

Katy and Freddie sidled into the front garden belonging to Katy's grandparents and breathed a sigh of relief. They drew the big bolt across the gate to stop anyone following them and went inside.

By the oven in the kitchen Sybil and Mouser were snoozing contentedly in their baskets. Grandma Rose was cooking mince pies for Freddie to take with him the next day when he visited Winston, his grandfather, at Whispering Pines, the residential home where he lived. Freddie's mum was going to send him with some books and Turkish delight too, one of his grandad's favourite treats. And Katy was going with Freddie on the bus.

Freddie's eyes were like saucers as he stared at the dragon in the wash basket and his curly hair nearly stood up on end.

'I can't believe it,' he said to himself. She was curled up in a blanket, but every so often her wings would vibrate with her snores and light would dance from the shimmering scales of her body. He started to speculate just how big she could get. They might have to move her to the shed in Grandpa Ron's garden or even the garage, but what if she got really enormous? Then, he had a brilliant idea, his dad worked at Exeter airport as a pilot, perhaps they had a spare airplane hangar? He started to work on the logistics of getting food there, they would probably have to use an articulated lorry, but how many times a day? When his thoughts were rudely interrupted.

'Well, what are we going to do?' Katy's voice suddenly intruded on his calculations. 'I mean I have tried to set her free but she doesn't seem to want to go. And now with all these reporters around. - By the way, why are they here? I know Mr Entwhistle is s'posed to be famous, but even so.'

'I think there was something on the news this morning,' Grandpa Ron volunteered. 'There's a German professor who doesn't seem to think too much of our next door neighbour and now the papers have got hold of it. Says he's a bit of an imposter. Oh and Rose did you see Marjory Farthing is alive! The professor rescued her after she had crash landed in a balloon on a cargo ship sailing from Sumatra to Belem. Once in Belem she got lost trying to find the airport and ended up in the Amazon jungle. Luckily Professor von Flusspferd found her just as she was about to eaten as a quick snack by a giant anaconda.'

'You think I've had time to watch the news when we've got dragons appearing willy-nilly all over the house?' answered Grandma Rose as she wiped flour from her nose. The mince pies were smelling absolutely delicious, luckily she said she thought Freddie and Katy should try one each to check they were tasty enough.

'And Katy, back to your question about what to do with your dragon, I think let nature take its course. Sooner or later that there dragon of yours will let you know what to do. Just keep her safe in the meantime.' said Grandma Rose very wisely.

The children nodded. But that could be easier said than done thought Freddie to himself, as later he dodged all the media vans and paraphernalia on the way back home. Goodness knows what would happen if the world found out about Sybil!

The next day late in the afternoon Katy and Freddie got ready to visit Freddie's grand-father Winston. Whispering Pines on the outskirts of the town was a very comfortable residential home and Freddie visited his grandfather there regularly. Grandma Rose gave them some of her mince pies piled into a tin decorated with snowmen. Freddie's backpack was heavy with books, as Winston had been a librarian and always had his nose in one. He was focusing on geography at the moment, he was interested in islands and archipelagos of the world, so Freddie's mum had put in books on Indonesian islands and the Nordenskjold Archipelago.

Katy had packed Sibyl into her blue backpack making sure that the dragon's eyes and nose had a gap where the flap came over the top, so that she could see, but not be seen. Grandpa Ron had said he thought it was too soon for the world to encounter an ice dragon just yet. The number 22 would take them to a bus stop almost immediately outside Whispering Pines, which suited them, as it was a cold, foggy day, and the damp seemed to seep through their jumpers and coats making them shiver.

Unbeknown to them they had been spotted emerging from the Clutterbuck house by Humphrey who, suitably disguised, had eluded the few remaining reporters outside his house and managed to tail the bus in his silver sports car, his protuberant eyes staring over the steering wheel in dogged determination, whilst his ginger moustache twitched irritably. The car with the rather conspicuous number plate, "HUM3" was now parked around the corner. He soon realised that they were going to visit the very building he was planning to buy and turn into luxury flats. Yet another black mark against them as far as he was concerned. He suspected that the dragon had gone with them, as the window next to Katy on the bus had been thick with ice crystals when she got off. He needed to get his hands on the creature ASAP!

As the children alighted and walked up the drive to the property, the bay trees standing in pots either side of the entrance were dripping, creating little puddles underneath and Katy seeing Sibyl reflected in one of them quickly drew her backpack flap a little tighter. They yanked the bell outside the large green door of the home, it jangled - echoing throughout the building and almost immediately the door was opened by gentleman with a bulbous red nose, wearing an apron.

'Hello Freddie, come to see your grandad?' the gentleman moved aside to let them into the house.

'How's tricks? Don't forget to sign yourselves in will you? Or Martha will have my guts for garters.'

Martha was the supervisor and owner of the home, the rest of the staff and most of the residents lived in trepidation in case they provoked her ire in some way or other. She had pink hair, stuck on top of her head in a bun, wore sparkly high heels and poured herself into the tightest clothes she could find which accentuated the very strange fact she had a very long body and very short legs with knees which never seemed to face the front.

The children dutifully signed the visitors' book, sniffing the delicious aroma of cooking dinner wafting from the kitchens. Whatever you might say, the home's owner certainly made sure that the residents got wholesome meals. They made their way through an enormous hallway and into the lounge where Freddie's grandad Winston sat with one of his friends playing chess. Another resident, Mrs Sweeting sat in the far corner, she was so tiny her feet in their slippers hardly touched the carpet edging the room. She looked very industrious with her knitting needles busily constructing the scaffolding of an enormous scarf. Two elderly men were sat dozing in front of the TV, one of them wearing odd socks.

'Hello Grandad.'

Winston's face lit up at the sight of Freddie and Katy. A huge grin spread itself across his countenance like the sun emerging from a rain laden cloud.

'Hello, hello my dears.' He turned to his chess partner.

'You remember Freddie don't you Charlie?'

'Of course I do, and who is this young lady?' Charlie asked looking at Katie who blushed pink.'Why this is Kat, she and Freddie are great pals aren't you?' The children nodded feeling slightly self-conscious as children tend to do at times in the presence of adults.

Winston spotted the cake tin Katy carried with her. She held it out to him.

'Well here's a treat – mince pies! No one bakes like Rose, I'm going to be very popular today!' Despite Winston's hearty voice booming through the room there was muted response.

The man with odd socks in front of the TV snored in agreement, his breath softly blowing the green, spikey fronds of the Christmas tree located next to his armchair while Mrs Sweeting in the far corner clicked her needles even faster.

Winston looked around the room and sighed heavily, things could certainly do with being a bit livelier. Apparently next week there would be a magician after Christmas lunch and there was an outing to the zoo on Boxing Day, but only if enough people put their names down on the list, so far only himself and Charlie had volunteered to go.

Freddie and Katy plonked themselves down on a plush, velvet sofa, its cushions enveloping them in its luxury. There was a small sneeze from Katy's backpack. Katy could feel a cold tingle on the back of her neck. What she couldn't see was that Sibyl's nose was wrinkled in dismay, the feathers the sofa was stuffed with were tickling her nostrils unmercifully, and another sneeze was working its way down the back of her throat.

'Aaatchoooo!!!'

Katy took one of Grandpa Ron's clean handkerchiefs out of her pocket and made a big show of blowing her nose. Ice was sticking her curls together at the nape of her neck, the collar of her jacket was stiff with crystals.

She put her backpack onto the parquet floor next to

the sofa, unaware that there was a small feather dancing around inside it threatening Sibyl's nose once again. Winston shivered pulling his cardigan tighter.

'Do you think they have the heating on Charlie?' he asked his friend.

'I dunno, t'is cold enough to freeze the feathers on a seagull in flight Winston,' replied his friend.

Mrs Sweeting knitted even faster and started to cast off the stitches on her vivid pink scarf, her feet clad in her purple pom-pom slippers bouncing up and down in rhythm to her knitting needles. She was certainly going to need it soon the way things were going, it seemed to be getting extraordinarily draughty. Freddie could see the dragon's breath had started to freeze the surface of the parquet flooring and gulped, perhaps bringing Sibyl here for an outing wasn't such a good idea.

One of the men sitting in front of the TV woke up with a start.

'Where am I? What's the time?' he asked in a confused voice.

'Whispering Pines Bert, and it is 5 o'clock,' answered

his friend with the odd socks who'd only just woken up himself, whose name happened to be Ravi.

'Oh, time for a sherry before dinner then.' Bert heaved himself out of his armchair and started to walk towards the sideboard where the sherry was kept. From Katy's backpack came another louder explosion, Katy buried her face in the handkerchief.

Ravi glanced at her. 'Nasty cold you've got there!'

Bert looked slightly surprised as his feet in their tartan slippers started to slip from under him.

'Here, what's going on?' He cried, but his feet had taken on a life of their own. He started to slide gracefully across the floor in slow motion and eventually landed, much to Mrs Sweeting's confusion, on her lap.

'I'm sorry Winifred, my legs aren't what they used to be,' he apologised. Mrs Sweeting twittered like a cheerful little wren as Bert tried to haul himself up off her knees. He kept grabbing the scarf which she had already wrapped around her neck, pulling it tighter and tighter, causing her to become redder and redder in the face.

'Oh my, Freddie,' Katy hissed at her friend, whilst frantically trying to push her blue backpack further and further behind the sofa with her foot.

They could both see the ice had formed what amounted to a skating rink in the middle of the room.

'Oh look,' Charlie nudged Winston and pointed to the Christmas tree, 'I don't remember those icicles when we decorated it last night.' It was true there were indeed icicles hanging down from the branches amongst the flashing lights and brightly coloured baubles. Just at that moment at the other end of the room Bert managed to extricate himself from the scarf and pulling Mrs Sweeting with him glided onto the floor. With effortless ease (or so it seemed) they swooped into each other's arms and pirouetted in the centre of the room. Mrs Sweeting twirled several times in an elegant impression of a reluctant swan, her arms waving delicately, whilst Bert gave a more forceful imitation of a walrus trying to flap onto some solid rocks.

'Hey, I say,' Ravi got up to help his friends, but within seconds had joined them in a skating display of unusual style and ingenuity.

'Well I don't know what's going on, but I'm not going to be left out.' Charlie stuffed a cushion down the back of his trousers, in case he landed on the ice, grabbed his walking stick from the side of his chair and turning it upside down slid onto the rink. He rescued the leftover wool yarn used by Mrs Sweeting that had bounced onto the floor, which had now frozen into a firm, flat ball and started to push it across the ice with his stick.

'Come on Winston, let's aim for under the tea table over there.'

'Grandad, don't you think it might be a little dangerous?' Freddie was getting really concerned now. How were they going to make sure that no one would get hurt?

'If you can't have a bit of fun at my age what has the world come to?' answered Winston. Freddie sighed and reluctantly handed him his walking stick. Like a couple of school boys Charlie and Winston slid this way and that, clashing walking sticks as they tried to get possession of the pink wool ball flying across the ice. With each step they became more confident. Come to think about it, Katy realised that Bert, Ravi and Mrs Sweeting were all beginning to look rather at home on the makeshift rink. They were all laughing, quite loudly in fact, and looked as if they were rather enjoying themselves.

The door at the far end of the lounge swung open as more residents started to arrive to see what was going on. The first in the queue was Mr Burtlesnap, who always wore a flat cap, indoors and out, whatever the weather. He was pushing his walking frame very sedately, followed by six others who were having a rather heated discussion over what went first on scones, jam or cream. Mr Burtlesnap looking like an aged tortoise stuck his head out from under his cap, staring unblinkingly at the scene in front of him.

Then slowly he turned his frame so the wheels made contact with the ice. The lady behind him called Mrs Blenkinsop grasped his waist to stop him, as she watched what was happening in front of her.

'Oh my, everyone has gone totally doolally! Please Mr Burtlesnap don't do anything foolish, you're 90 years old for goodness sake,' she gasped in alarm.

Mr Burtlesnap scowled, he had never liked being told what to do and always made a point of doing the exact opposite. With that he launched himself onto the frozen wasteland of the parquet floor, one by one the residents behind him grabbed on to each other like a weird, ancient, giant caterpillar.

They meandered, zigzagging across the ice with ever gathering speed. Some of them started giggling, soon the giggles became chuckles and very quickly the chuckles became raucous laughter which wafted through Whis

pering Pines up into the higher echelons where Martha the supervisor sat in her office painting her nails with red sparkly nail varnish. Her eyebrows raised in annoyance as she heard noises getting louder and louder.

They sounded far too happy to be at her establishment, she preferred muted voices and fearful whispers, which assured her that all were under her thumb. She stood up, straightened her dress and made for the office door.

Meanwhile the rosy-cheeked cook in the Whispering Pines' kitchen had finished dishing up the roast dinner piled onto plates and put it all on the serving trolley. Mike, one of the helpers, was wheeling the trolley along the corridor with some difficulty, as one of the wheels was loose, towards the dining room. He could hear laughter coming from the lounge, and had a little grin, as laughter is catching as we all know, just like yawning and chickenpox. Why not take a short cut he thought to himself. He was intrigued to find out what was going on as everyone was always usually so quiet, it was nice to hear them so jolly.

He opened the door pushing the rickety trolley in front of him. With a slick movement the front of the trolley became hooked in Bert's braces, who was at the back of the human caterpillar and with one motion Mike and the dinner trolley joined him. They careered around the icy floor, narrowly missing Winston who had just scored a goal at the tea table, and Katy who was sat with her hands over her eyes. All of a sudden Mike and the trolley swerved dangerously and with a twang detached themselves from Bert and hurtled towards the door at the end of the lounge. In the blink of any eye it opened to reveal Martha, looking extremely stern. She was just about to give everyone a good ticking off for unruly behaviour when a Yorkshire pudding, 2 sprouts, 3 carrots and a jug of gravy landed over her head. And as she had taken a deep breath to project her voice above the noise a roast potato landed in her open mouth, while thick gravy cascaded down the front of her dress. Everyone else fell into a heap in the middle of the floor, but as they looked around it soon dawned on them they could be in a lot of trouble.

The whole room went silent.

Then an odd thing happened - because Martha had caught sight of herself in the massive mirror hanging at the opposite end of the room. At first the sound was rather muffled, but once Mike had helped her get the potato out of her mouth it turned into a great roar. No one could understand what the noise was, but suspected it could mean a rumpus. Winston looked at Charlie, Mrs Sweeting looked at Bert, and Ravi looked at a stray carrot teetering on the top of Mrs Blenkinsop's blue rinse chignon.

To Katy and Freddie's amazement they realised Martha was laughing. Years of stress managing a money-losing residential home had taken its toll and the last few months trying to stop Humphrey Entwhistle from snaffling it from under her nose had made it all worse, but now the real Martha bubbled to the surface. She laughed and laughed till tears made streaks in the gravy plastered all over her face.

Suddenly everyone was laughing with her. Katy, unseen by anyone else but Freddie, got Sibyl to breathe gently from the backpack to gradually melt the ice from the floor. Mike got a mop to wipe up the water and Winston and Charlie used some tea towels to tidy the gravy and vegetables from Martha.

Meanwhile unsuspected by anyone, Humphrey Entwhistle had ensconced himself outside in the garden by the window next to the sofa that Katy and Freddie were sat upon and had very quietly raised the bottom sash. He was wearing a dark woolly balaclava to hide his identity and was waiting for the first opportunity to scrobble Katy's backpack from behind the sofa. But as if by instinct the ice dragon's head turned and her eyes stared at him from beneath the backpack flap as he stretched out a greedy hand to grab it. She twitched her tail and gave an enormous sneeze directed right into his face, immediately freezing his balaclava to his moustache and eyebrows. He stumbled backwards and with a huge splash ended up in the garden pond, greatly surprising the fish nonchalantly swimming in an area they had always considered to be exclusive to them.

'What on earth was that?' Martha, quickly recovered, dashed over to the open window.

'Looked like a burglar to me!' Winston gazed suspiciously into the garden where Humphrey was sat in the middle of the pond in his dark clothes. It was getting very dimpsy now, but Winston could just make out the outline of the devious, but thwarted, dragon hunter.

'Here,' Charlie shouted, 'what do you think you're doing?' He threw a large cushion at Humphrey just as he was struggling out of the pond and knocked him back into it.

'Ring the police, ring the police,' Mrs Blenkinsop urged from the side lines. Mr Burtlesnap hadn't enjoyed things this much in a long while. He was scooting with speed towards the front door of the home using his walking frame in order to apprehend the suspected miscreant. He was fully armed with one of Mrs Sweeting's knitting needles and a makeshift bow made from one of his sock garters. Sadly though, just as Mr Burtlesnap had managed to fumble with the handle of the large green door to open it, Humphrey had escaped. With a huge effort and with the help of a tree branch drooping over the water, he had managed to pull himself up and make his escape shivering and dripping down the drive back to his car, evading the suspicious looks of passers-by.

But he hadn't been so fast that he escaped unscathed. Mr Burtlesnap was gratified by a loud yelp as he fired the knitting needle at Humphrey's retreating backside, shaking his fist in triumph, the ghost of a smile quivering at the edges of his mouth. Turning to join the others in the dining room for dinner he made two important decisions; one, he would ask his millionaire son to bail the home out and two, perhaps he would put his name down for the visit to the zoo on Boxing Day after all!

As it was time for his grandad to have dinner Freddie and Katy said goodbye to all their friends at Whispering Pines.

'Don't forget the Christingle service on Christmas Eve, Grandad,' Freddie reminded Winston.

'No, don't you worry we're all coming on the minibus for a bit of carol singing at the church, see you there. Not long to Christmas now!' Winston grinned at the children and waved to them as they left.

No, not long now. Katy shifted the backpack on her shoulders, it was starting to feel heavier as if Sybil was having another growing spurt. How much bigger was she going to get? And even more urgently who had been in the garden of Whispering Pines spying on them? Katy had a horrible feeling she thought she knew and her suspicions were confirmed when Freddie nudged her, as a silver sports car went roaring past them with "HUM3" on the number plate driven by someone in a black balaclava. As they stood waiting for the bus to go home Katy had a feeling of dread in the pit of her stomach. If Humphrey Entwhistle really was in trouble, how better to regain a lost reputation than to steal an ice dragon and claim he had discovered it himself?

Chapter 7. The Christmas Fair

T he Clutterbucks' neighbour sat in front of his bathroom mirror. His face was plastered in moisturising cream, as he had spent two hours the night before trying to remove his bala-clava, which had been frozen to his face by that nasty little brute of a dragon. It had not been a success. He had pulled off most of one eyebrow and half his moustache with it. His face was even pinker than usual and the ice hadn't seemed to melt very quickly at all, it clearly wasn't normal. How could a creature which had once looked so fragile be so horribly vindictive, he thought to himself, completely ignoring the fact he had been about to pinch Sybil for his own gain.

He had managed to stop the hordes of reporters hounding him outside his house by promising an exclusive interview to a well-known TV channel on Christmas morning in two days' time. He was due to open a Christmas Fair at the local school today, the biggest drawback being that it would be full of school children, the little blighters, he thought, forgetting he was once one himself. However it might just put him in everyone's good books again if he could pull it off without too many hitches. Should be easy enough, if only he could draw in his missing eyebrow, sadly the other half of his moustache would have to go. Why hadn't he been able to grab the dragon at the bookshop? It would have made things so much simpler, but then he hadn't known just how important the little "insect" was then although he had seen its potential right away. The problem was how was he going to get hold of it? The Clutterbucks were keeping the dragon a secret, so once he had it no one would be any the wiser that he hadn't been the one to find it all along, it would be his word against theirs and he was a celebrity.

His face suddenly brightened. A sinister thought came into his head, what if he bought some kind of dragon trap? It would have to be a biggish one as the creature seemed to be growing very fast. Humphrey went into his study and opened the laptop on his desk. It would be useless searching for "dragon traps", so what would be the nearest thing? Something it couldn't escape from, a net, a cage? And he would have to find something that a dragon would find irresistible to lure it inside - that would be a lot more difficult he realised. Humphrey rubbed his hands in glee. 'Ha! Just let that Clutterbuck girl and her wretched friend try and stop me now!' he thought to himself.

Grandma Rose was tut-tutting as she put the kettle on for morning tea, she couldn't see Mouser in his basket to begin with, as Sybil had grown in the night and had overflowed out of her basket into his. The cat peered out grumpily from underneath the dragon, one ear twitching in irritation, not at all happy. Sybil, however, snorted gentle dragon snores, deep in contentment, but Katy's grandma could see there may be a problem developing very soon, as at this rate the dragon may be having to move out of the house after a week and then where would it go? Not only that, the rest of the family were coming down soon, Christmas morning in fact and how were they all going to fit in? The dragon could be much bigger in two days' time and she was also worried about what Katy had said involving Humphrey Entwhistle. Grandma Rose had always been suspicious of the strange "happenings" that seemed to start after they had refused to sell their house to him. Ron had been much more trusting and refused to believe their neighbour could have been acting out of spite.

Angelic yuletide carols floated out from her radio and Rose sighed with relief, at least Ruthie was on the mend and out of hospital, so whatever happened next it would be a good Christmas, of that she was sure.

In the afternoon Rose and Katy were going to meet Freddie and his family at the Highbury School Christmas Fair. Katy could see that Sybil was getting bored, she had been scuttling up and down the stairs and breathing icicles all over the house, but Katy didn't really know what sorts of activities would keep a dragon occupied and out of mischief. So she very daringly suggested to her grandma that they took Sybil with them. There was a fancy dress competition taking place at the school and Katy was convinced they could smuggle the dragon in without anyone being the wiser. It would be very busy, there would be crowds of people dressed up to take part, and it would also be dark before they went home. Rose very reluctantly agreed. Katy had found a cat costume in an old dressing up box in the attic, her father had used it in a school pantomime many years before as Puss-in-Boots although she had to wear her own wellington boots as his were too big. Ron would drop them off in the car. Mouser had looked a little startled when she had appeared in the kitchen wearing her costume, obviously worried he was about to be replaced until she gave him a reassuring cuddle. Sybil wore a coat over her "costume" to make her brilliant scales less obvious and off they went a little late.

The school hall was beautifully bright, a large Christmas tree stood by the stage and garlands were hanging from the ceiling. There were many stalls selling toys, crackers, Christmas cakes and homemade sweets amongst other things. There were tree decorations and pottery that the children had made; jams, pickles, games like pin the tail on the reindeer, where you could win a prize of a selection box if you got your tail pinned closest to the right place. And at the far end of the hall was a small football goal, decorated as Santa's workshop. You could have three shots and if you got them all in you could win a coconut. No one batted an eyelid at Sybil, as to be fair, there were a lot of strange animals, princesses, knights, super heroes and mythical beasts squeezed in between the many tables of Christmas ware. Katy spotted Freddie and his family stood by the stage where one of the teachers was trying to make herself heard.

'Hello everyone! Yes we do have a Father Christmas a little later, no he's not the real one but one of his deputies Amy.' This was in reply to a query from Freddie's sister.

'However sadly what we don't have is the bouncy castle which was going on the field outside. The lorry has broken down so they are unable to get here on time.'

At this there was a collective groan from the parents who had bribed their children to come by promising them a turn on one.

'I hope you all have a lovely time nevertheless and we are going to start with the school choir singing Jingle Bells.' The teacher whose name happened to be Miss Hubbard sat at the piano and with a wave of her hand the choir burst into song.

Rose and Katy managed to jostle their way to the stage. Freddie's mum Grace was trying to explain to Amy why the real Father Christmas couldn't come and why there would not be a bouncy castle. The little girl was dressed as Spiderman and stood with her arms folded and a scowl upon her face. Freddie was dressed as the wolf from Red Riding Hood, (actually secretly it was a werewolf, but he didn't tell Amy). He'd made a rather good head out of papier-mache and stuck some whiskers on it made from pipe-cleaners, which were a rarity, as nowadays not many people smoke pipes. Luckily the fact he was wearing a wolf's head prevented Katy from seeing the expression on his face when he noticed Sybil with her.

'But I was looking forward to the bouncy castle Mum!' Amy grunted at her mother.

'But love, there are plenty of other things to do here, don't spoil it,' her mum replied.

'Yes Amy, I've seen you kicking balls in the garden, why don't you have a go at the goal game?' joined in Grandma Rose. Amy gave a faint smile and was on the point of agreeing when she noticed Sybil standing next to her.

'Who's that?' she pointed at the dragon in the green coat. Sybil's tail twitched, the scales on it flashed, reflecting the Christmas tree lights, she stood head and shoulders above Amy.

'Ooooh, I love your costume! Have you got wings?'

'Sorry,' Katy said hastily. 'She can't answer you very easily as she's got a sore throat.'

'Oh, but I love your tail.' Sybil's limpid green eyes stared into Amy's.

'C'mon,' Amy grabbed Sybil's coat sleeve with one claw in it. 'Let's try the football.' Sybil seemed quite happy to be pulled through the throng of people filling the hall.

Everyone else followed them. Rose was quite right, Amy won a coconut after scoring three goals in quick succession, although she complained that she didn't actually like coconuts, but Freddie said he did so that was alright. Katy could tell Freddie was dying to take her to one side to ask why she had brought the dragon with her. Amy took them proudly to a table where the Reception Class were selling Christmas decorations they had made, she pointed out a snowman she had designed to hang on the tree. Her mum bought it, as it was very originally wearing a Spiderman mask. It was as they were standing by the fudge and sweet stand, that Freddie took his chance to speak with Katy.

'You do know that Humphrey Entwhistle opened the school fair don't you? He could still be here.'

Katy gulped, it had never occurred to her that their next door neighbour might be there. She looked around in a panic, surely he would have been in a hurry to get away?

What neither Katy nor Freddie realised was that Humphrey had already spotted them and had quickly formed a plan.

He was at that very moment heavily disguising himself as the school Father Christmas. The role was originally going to be the headmaster's. Humphrey had soon changed that, Mr Throgmorton, the headmaster, had been thrust into a cleaning cupboard without ever seeing his assailant and secured there by a broom across the door. No one would hear Mr Throgmorton thumping on the door as there was so much noise already. In addition no one would recognise Humphrey in a red, padded costume and an enormous amount of white beard and very handily no one would question him carrying a huge red sack. It hadn't been planned, but unexpectedly fate had suddenly handed him an ideal chance for getting his hands on the dragon.

Meanwhile unaware of impending danger, they'd all had a go on the lucky dip barrel after Amy had eventually decided on chocolate fudge. They had also admired some beautiful, pottery pendants and brooches that had been lovingly made by Freddie's class.

'Which ones did you make?' asked Katy.

Freddie pointed to a couple of brooches, one with a mermaid on it and one with a unicorn, the detail on them was astonishing.

'They're lovely Freddie.'

Freddie grinned, Rose bought one and his mum bought the other, after all they were rather splendid and absolutely unique.

And now, much to Amy's delight the imposter Father Christmas was sat on the stage. Humphrey hadn't intended to be sat on the stage. He had emptied most of the presents from his sack into three, handy, unused tea urns and was about to search for Sybil when Miss Hubbard had found him in the corridor outside the hall.

'Come on Reginald, you're late,' she had chided him laughingly, thinking she was talking to the headmaster. He had unwillingly followed her onto the stage.

'Now children, who wants to see Father Christmas? Queue at the bottom of the steps, show your ticket to the Christmas Elf and then you can have your turn.'

Humphrey swallowed uncomfortably. How long before his ruse would be discovered? How did you make five presents go between a zillion children and how did you stop a mob of disgruntled youngsters setting on you when they realised you did only have five presents?

Due to nifty elbow work Amy had pushed to the front of the queue and was stomping up the steps towards him. The determined look on her face did not bode well.

'Hello, my name is Amy and I want a Spiderman car, but one you can sit on,' she announced looking at the almost-empty sack suspiciously.

'Amy, most toys on your list come on Christmas Day,' her mother Grace said quickly. 'Father Christmas just has little gifts today.'

'Huh,' Amy glanced down the steps at Sybil.

'My friend is shy, she wants to come up with me,' and before Katy or Freddie could stop her she went to the bottom of the steps, grabbed Sybil by the sleeve and hauled her on to the stage. Sybil however wasn't fooled by the Father Christmas outfit and started to struggle to get away.

'Don't be shy, don't be shy,' cooed Amy at her new friend.

'Ho ho ho! Oh dear, I've left some presents on the side of the stage,' Humphrey hoped his voice was sufficiently disguised. 'Why doesn't your friend help me find them?' he said.

Amy anxious to get her present quickly nodded and thrust Sybil out into the wings of the stage, whereupon Humphrey quickly followed and behind the curtains whipped the sack over the dragon and swung it over his shoulder. He ran down the steps and out into the corridor. There was a brief pause whilst everyone waited for him to reappear, but after a minute or two ticked by people started to realise something was wrong. A little boy who was waiting started to wail, refusing to be comforted by the Christmas Elf who herself was looking rather bewildered. Katy turned very pale, she had a horrible feeling they had all been tricked and she was pretty sure by whom. She and Freddie looked at one another and leaping onto the stage, they handed a grumpy Amy to her mother and gave chase.

The bag on Humphrey's back wriggled as Sybil tried to escape, her tail thrashed against the sack and her claws started to rip it apart. Humphrey had no inkling of what a dragon's rage can do when they are cornered. By the time they had reached outside onto the field in front of the car park Sybil had torn a hole big enough to fall through. She landed on the ground her emerald eyes blazing, taking a huge breath, she blew a great blast of cold air lifting Humphrey into the sky like an Arctic hurricane. The freezing air swirled around and around, until ice formed to make a big frozen tower. It had a pointed turret at the top and a slide, like a white, twisted, crystalline snake formed all the way to the bottom. Humphrey meanwhile had landed on the roof of the school building such was the force of the dragon blast and Sybil landed next to him, her tail swishing like an angry cat's.

Sensing something was afoot and anxious to see what was going on a small crowd of people soon swarmed out of the school doors onto the field, led by Freddie and Katy.

'Wow, I thought they said there wasn't a bouncy castle?' said one of the dads.

'Well it's not a bouncy castle is it?' said his wife, 'It's a helter-skelter.' And sure enough that is exactly what it looked like.

'But where are the steps to get to the top?' asked one practical child.

'Perhaps we could use the ones in the library?' replied an ingenious Year 5 pupil.

Katy and Freddie scanned the area around them for Sybil. Perhaps she really had flown away now thought Katy. The idea gave her a jolt. But then Freddie pointed to the school roof. There, hidden in the shadows, they could just make out the dragon's outline, but only because they knew what they were looking for.

Luckily in the meantime Miss Hubbard had found the headmaster in the cleaning cupboard. Using some improvisation and an old rather moth-eaten Father Christmas outfit stored on top of a school bookcase, along with the presents that had been found when the school caretaker had gone to fetch an extra tea urn, service at the school fair was resumed. In fact it was rather better now, as they could charge everyone 50p to go on the ice helter-skelter. It conveniently melted overnight so there was nothing to clear up the next day either and in case anyone is interested, Mabel Tootinghorn won the fancy dress competition. By a strange twist of fate she was disguised as a dragon.

Later on Mr Throgmorton told the police sergeant who came to take his statement that the only reason he believed he had been locked in the cupboard and impersonated was so that the thief could steal the Highbury School tug-of-war trophy. Luckily the little girl dressed as a dragon on stage (Sybil) had been reported as found safe and sound, her kidnap had obviously been used as a distraction and all was well in the end. However the school planned to have an alarm installed after the holidays just in case.

But of the thief the police could find no sign. Only Freddie and Katy realised that Humphrey must be trapped on the roof covered in ice next to Sybil. There wasn't much they could do about it so they made their way home. Sybil appeared sometime later at the Clutterbucks' home when the coast was clear. She had defrosted Humphrey slightly before flying from the roof of the school building and left him to find his own way down the fire escape.

'Who was that girl dressed up that Amy took a shine

to?' Freddie's mum asked him later.

'Oh that was Sybil, someone Katy knows,' he answered more or less truthfully.

'Well, we must have her over for tea one day,' his mum replied.

It was Christmas Eve morning, Katy sat in bed holding the snow globe she had bought from the tree farm. She shook it watching the tiny snow-flakes drift around the palace inside. Then she wound the key and listened to the tinkling tune it made. Her grandma popped her head around the bedroom door.

'I've just heard from your mum, they will all be down

tomorrow and send their love. Ruthie is much better now and looking forward to seeing you soon.' Grandma stopped for a moment and listened to the music.

'Do you know, I think it's playing the Carol of the Bells,' she said, 'I seem to remember it's based on an old Ukrainian folk chant. It's lovely. Anyhow, breakfast is almost ready if you want some.' She went over to the bedroom window.

'Oh my! I wondered where Sybil had gone as she wasn't in the kitchen.'

Katy leapt off her bed and peered out of the curtains. There under the pine tree with the violet cones lay Sybil, she had crept out there as the warmth of the house no longer suited her. She had grown bigger again, and was now the size of a large deer. All around the garden was a hoar frost, icicles hung from the trees and the lawn was carpeted with a thick sheet of rime. Sybil slowly raised her head and looked at Katy. Never had Katy seen a look of such misery. But stranger than anything else was the melting of the scales upon the dragon's body. Like waves of water they shimmered in the rising sunlight, rippled, then seem to vanish so that Katy could hardly see Sybil at all. She was almost translucent, but just visible, pale colours in the strands of ice decorating the garden reflected on her body. What was happening to her? At times the dragon disappeared altogether, as if Katy was looking into an empty mirror.

'Oh dear,' she doesn't look happy does she? It's a good job not many people can see behind our house, otherwise some busybody would be on the phone to the fire brigade or some such. Not that I know as I could blame them seeing a dragon in our back garden,' Grandma Rose added reasonably.

'I wish I knew what to do with an ice dragon, it's not as if I've made her stay here. She could have left at any time.' Katy said dismally.

'Yes,' replied her grandma, 'but perhaps she feels an attachment to you. After all if it wasn't for you some bird would have gobbled her up when she was very tiny.'

Katy realised there could be some truth in what Rose said, and it might mean that Sybil would need some encouragement to go and discover where she really belonged. If she was with them much longer they would have to explain her to more and more people and not everyone might have her best interests at heart.

A bit later as she ate her breakfast she spotted headlines in the local newspaper.

"Famous explorer Humphrey Entwhistle to join Professor von Flusspferd in local TV debate on Christmas morning."

Grandpa Ron saw her reading it and chuckled.

'That should cause a few fireworks!' he said. 'They can't stand each other and now Marjory Farthing has turned up there is going to be an investigation into how she ended up in a balloon over the Pacific Ocean, unreported by our famous neighbour who was in Sumatra with her at the time.'

Katy looked at the photograph of Professor von Flusspferd. He had very twinkling eyes and a kind smile. She made up her mind immediately that if she got the opportunity she would try to ask him what to do about Sybil, after all the paper did say he was a conservationist and loved animals. The paper also explained that, as he would be in Devon for the TV interview, he was going to attend the Christingle service at the local church, because it just so happened the organist Miss Hubbard was his niece. Katy remembered that she was the music teacher at Highbury School too.

Sybil seemed to have lost her appetite and wouldn't come into the house anymore with any amount of persuasion, she preferred to stay in her cold den out in the garden. She put her head in Katy's lap and let Katy stoke her neck, but after a while Sybil pushed her away with her nose and slumped in a sorrowful heap again.

Katy had been feeling despondent herself, but she had been thinking very hard and felt a lot better now because she had a plan.

'Don't worry Sybil, we'll sort something out,' she whispered into the dragon's ear.

Unbeknownst to Katy, Humphrey Entwhistle had also made a plan, but his was a lot more wicked. He had been secretly recording Sybil's snores and sighs as she slept. He had taken delivery of a large cage early in the morning and intended to put the recording inside the prison to lure her into it, hopefully thinking there was another dragon inside. Taking note of the fact that Sybil had been eating a mince pie the day before in the garden, he planned to put six pies he had bought from the supermarket in there too for good measure, not realising that Grandma Rose baked far superior ones.

He hadn't had a good night's sleep however, as Marjory Farthing and Professor von Flusspferd had come down the day before and Humphrey was terrified that he would bump into them before Christmas Day, which was when he planned to reveal his latest discovery which was of course going to be Sybil.

He also had a sneaking feeling that Marjory had been outside his home last night, as he kept waking up thinking he heard the cry of the Sumatran Rhinoceros, which was how they used to call to each other in the jungle if they became separated.

He had heard the Clutterbucks talking about going to the church for the Christingle service, he was pretty sure they wouldn't be taking the dragon with them as she was so big now, so that was when he would leap into action.

The day seemed to go very slowly. The hour hand was reluctant to move or so it seemed to Humphrey, however Katy was very busy and the time seemed to whizz by for her.

She wrapped Christmas presents, finished garlanding the house with holly and ivy, and helped her grandma ice and decorate the Christmas cake. By five o'clock it was time to go to the church where they would meet Freddie and his family - and Winston would be arriving with his friends from the residential home in the minibus.

Within half an hour they had all met up in the church car park surrounded by lots of chattering children and their exhausted parents. Winston was carrying the books that Freddie had given to him a few days ago.

'I really loved these,' he said to Freddie and his mum as he handed the books back to them.

'Did you know that scientists first recorded information on Komodo dragons properly around 1910? They're found on four Indonesian islands, one of them is called Komodo. You wouldn't think there could still be dragons around and not just in fairy tales.' He said jokingly. Katy tried not to catch her grandparents' eyes and especially avoided Freddie's.

'This other book on the Nordenskjold Archipelago, I let Charlie read,' he added.

'Yes, I don't think you'll find much there, it's iced up most of the time 'cos it's near Siberia, a bit boring really,' his friend said.

Once they all managed to squeeze through the huge wooden church doors they all sat expectantly in the pews. Excited children prattled, waiting. They knew that the most important moment of the service would be the lighting of the candles on their Christingles and the singing of "Away in a Manger", which never failed to bring a tear to Grandma Rose's eye. Huge candles were lit in the alcoves in front of the stained glass windows, a magnificent Christmas tree reached tall, almost into the rafters of the church ceiling and everyone shuffled their carol sheets in anticipation of a good old sing-song.

There was a hushed silence as Miss Hubbard took her seat at the church organ, foot on pedal, ready to burst into "Once in Royal David's City". Katy gazed intently along the pews to see if she could spot Professor von Flusspferd. He was perched on a seat, near the front by the Christmas tree. With great aplomb Miss Hubbard placed her fingers upon the keys, but when she pressed them the sound which emerged was not what most people were expecting. If you think about a choir of cats joined at times by the baying of a moose, you will have some idea of the noise which filled the church. Miss Hubbard looked at her fingers in horror, perhaps they were playing tricks on her, but no - it was indeed the church organ which had let her down, much to her excruciating embarrassment. Looking around she could see most of the audience had their fingers in their ears.

'Oh dear!' the vicar looked at his congregation apologetically.

'We seem to have a technical hitch. To be fair it is a very old instrument and we don't use it every Sunday.' He was puzzled, he had known about the leak from the ceiling which had caused some rust, and possibly contributed to the terrible discord, but he knew nothing about the church mice who had decided to take up residence inside some of the pipes and were the real cause of the problem.

People were just starting to get restless and the children to complain, when there was a great rush of cold wind which pushed the wooden doors of the church open again, filling it with an icy sigh. The candles upon the window sills flickered and battled to stay alight as people pulled their coats tighter around them. Suddenly there was the sound of scratching on the church roof above them. The vicar looked very sternly at the verger who was supposed to have dealt with the rats in the belfry.

'Cooo, look at the Christmas tree!' A little voice piped up from the pew in front of them. Everyone looked and gasped in astonishment, the tree was draped with icicles of all sizes. They rattled together, chiming with a cacophony of musical notes as they moved in the sighing breeze left by the open doors.

'Well goodness gracious me!' exclaimed the vicar, and because he was a quick thinking vicar he handed Miss Hubbard a small mallet from a box of children's toys kept under a pew near the font. 'I wonder if this might help us out,' he said.

Miss Hubbard gently tapped the icicle nearest to her

which gave off a clear, true note. A bit like an orchestra tuning up before a concert, she tested her new instrument until she felt confident and then with a nod of her head everyone burst into their first carol.

Katy and Freddie were having a fierce whispered debate behind their carol sheet.

'Sybil must be on the church roof,' Katy hissed frantic with worry. 'We need to get Professor von Flusspferd so we can ask him what to do.'

Freddie had not heard about Katy's plan before. 'Why, what can he do?' he hissed back.

'Freddie, please just do as I ask. He is a really famous zoologist and I trust him more than Mr Entwhistle that's for sure.'

'Ok,' Freddie agreed. He could see that the professor was singing heartily but he didn't have a carol sheet. Freddie grabbed a spare one from the pew and quickly made his way to where the professor stood.

'Excuse me sir,' he whispered from behind it to the professor, 'we have an emergency which I believe only you can help us with.' The professor looked extremely puzzled.

'Only I can help you viz?' he whispered back.

'Yes, we are having problems with an extremely un-usual pet on the roof of the church. I believe we may have to climb up the bell tower.'

'Vot??' the professor frowned, was this some silly joke he wondered. But then his niece Miss Hubbard saw Fred-die and smiled.

'You know my niece?'

'Yes she is our music teacher at school.' Freddie replied.

'Alright, but be varned, if zis is a silly prank I shall not be amuzed!'

Luckily at this point the singing had finished and in the shuffling about of people taking their seats again Katy joined them as they slipped into the vestry where the steps to the bell tower were situated. Luckily the bell ringers weren't using it until midnight to chime in Christ-mas day and so the way was clear for them.

'Hurry please,' she gasped as they climbed the stone steps twisting and turning, higher and higher.

At the top of the tower the windows were quite high and had no glass. They stood on tiptoe to look out, below them stood the town lit up in miniature, above them stars twinkled in the velvet night sky.

The professor looked around him.

'Vere is dis animal?' he asked.

'OH!' Freddie exclaimed in dismay as he leaned out of the tower, Katy grabbed onto his jacket and grasped the granite edge of the window frame. The professor followed the gaze of the two children out on to the roof. All he could see were slates and stone gargoyles. But then one of the gargoyles seemed to move, the body shifting in the pale light had the moon and stars reflected in its scales, until it vanished merging into the night, now almost invisible.

Soundless, Sybil crouched there and clinging to her tail was Humphrey Entwhistle.

Humphrey's plot had not gone according to plan. True he had managed to record Sybil and pop the recording into the cage with the mince pies to try and trap her, but he had not listened to the whole recording, there was more on it than he realised. So when Marjory Farthing arrived at his house at 6 o'clock in the evening uninvited, she heard the plaintive singing of the Sumatran rhinoceros coming from Humphrey's wintry, dark garden and went to investigate. Sybil also heard the mournful cry and being a soft hearted dragon, went to see what was happening by flying over the garden hedge.

Humphrey, who was hiding behind a sundial warmly dressed in his thermal underwear in case there was a long night of waiting, saw Marjory blunder into the cage and fall on to six mince pies, but he was too late to stop the door sliding down and locking, trapping her inside.

Sybil landed on top of the cage, and was peering inside it at an anxious Marjory, who could only see the strange outline of a rather large animal sniffing at her through the bars. Humphrey realised he could not miss what might be his last chance at capturing the dragon. She was getting far too big for the Clutterbucks to hide much longer and he was determined not to be thwarted yet again. He began to climb up the cage and slide along the top to where he thought Sybil was sat. But she hardly seemed to exist anymore. One minute she was a solid creature sitting on top of his trap and the next she melted from his view into the dusky night.

'Was she starting to become invisible?' he wondered. In which case he really could not afford to fail this time, as she might disappear altogether before too long. Sybil snorted in alarm and looked behind her, seeing Humphrey crawling towards her, she started to flap her wings gradually lifting from the cage. Humphrey grabbed her tail just as she shot up into the moonlit sky, leaving behind Marjory who had been too astonished to say a word, abandoned in the prison which had been intended for the dragon.

Sybil with her sensitive nose had unerringly caught the scent of the one person she could trust as she flew through the air. She followed it to the church and once landing on the roof she proceeded to sniff around her peering this way and that to find Katy.

Now Humphrey swung from Sybil's tail, precariously dangling from the church roof. His ginger hair floated in the wind which was whipped up around the steeple and his legs in their thermal underwear felt strangely numb.

'Achhh, mein gootness!' Professor von Flusspferd's jaw

dropped, he had travelled all over the world, but never had he seen a creature like the one sitting on the roof before him. Not only that, but he wasn't too sure how long Humphrey Entwhistle was going to be able to hang on to its tail. Much as he disliked the man he didn't want him falling to a sticky end in the church car park.

'What should we do?' Katy asked him in a panicky voice.

'Vell first of all ve must try to get the gentleman clinging to her tail to safety.'

'Yes but how?' Freddie could see that Humphrey's knuckles were white with holding on and his teeth were clenched with exertion.

'Vell if the animal trusts you, you must coax her along the ledge to zis vindow.'

Katy leaned out carefully, 'Sybil,' she called softly, 'Sybil come on, we're here now.'

Sybil slowly lifted her head, she shook her scales, each one seeming to flash reflected stars, Humphrey's feet clattered against the stone wall below the roof as she moved. Icicles draped the church guttering, the ledge outside was shimmering with a frosty coating. She stared at Katy, Freddie and the professor, her expression was a warning and all three realised that she was about to take flight from the church roof again.

'You haf no time children, her instincts are strong she vishes to find her home. Entvistle you must let go, grab zee edge or she vill take you vis her.' The professor's voice raised in alarm as Katy scrambled through the stone frame of the open window, closely followed by Freddie. They edged inch by inch towards the dragon.

'Vot are you doing - come back it is too dangerous!'

'I can't let her go on her own,' Katy's voice drifted back to him on the night air. 'She's only a week old.'

Humphrey watched them in terror, his arms were aching and he did not dare look down. The idea of letting go of the dragon's tail was impossible, his hands felt glued to it in fright.

Professor von Flusspferd started to climb out onto the roof himself, he couldn't let these children go by themselves, he was used to perilous situations and could help. However he was just too late. The two children had clambered onto Sybil's back and even now as the professor watched helplessly, the dragon launched into the scintillating night sky. Far below the coloured lights around the town harbour twinkled, cosy and inviting, but a cold wind whistled above them. It came from the north and it was singing a strange song only Sybil could understand.

Her wings beat steadily through the darkness. Where only bats or owls would normally wander the twilight, she would travel. She had suddenly felt something calling her and its call was too strong to ignore, her instincts were telling her to go north and like an invisible string those instincts pulled her onwards.

Professor von Flusspferd scrambled back inside the tower of the church. What was he going to tell the families of these children? And what of the extraordinary dragon? It was there one minute and then not there the next. How could that be? He shook his head, the only thing to do now was to speak to his niece. She obviously knew at least one of the children so perhaps that way he could find the family and describe what had happened. But then how was he going to explain the fact that the children had vanished taking to the air on a dragon? And how was he going to explain the fact that Humphrey Entwhistle wouldn't be able to take part in the TV programme the next day, because he too had been whisked north by a mythical beast?

It was very cold swinging from a dragon's tail as it flew.

Sybil was struggling to climb higher into the sky as she was being thrown off balance with the extra weight of Humphrey clinging to it. Katy shouted to him, the wind tearing at her voice.

'You have to get on to Sybil's back, or we might all fall from the sky,' she yelled at him. Humphrey's face shone back at her in the moonlight, white and petrified, but he managed to nod. Slowly he moved, hand over hand along the dragon's tail until he was able to climb onto her back helped by Freddie. They all clung together, friend and foe as the dragon winged her way over the darkened land and her passengers could see the red cliffs of Devon fading away behind them as Sybil soared above the sea. Moonbeams slid across the rolling waves, like search lights peering into the depths to see if the creatures beneath were still sleeping. Seahorses, turtles, crabs, oysters, dolphins - a treasure-trove of ocean life slumbering under the searching fingers of the night's reflected sun.

Freddie felt the wind whistle past his ears, luckily both the children were wearing their winter coats and shoes, but this did not stop their noses turning red with cold. Freddie clung tighter to Katy's waist and Katy clung to

Sybil's neck. She had no idea where they were going, but the rhythm of the dragon's pulsing wings and the warmth of her body lulled Katy into a doze. Freddie however strained to see what was ahead, soon they were over land again and his eyes gradually got used to seeing in the gloom. He could make out valleys and mountains, rivers softly snaking their way northwards; then small towns, and big cities bright with light hiding the canopy of the stars.

Eventually though the air grew clear and crisp. After what seemed like hours, gone were cities, towns or even tiny villages. In their place stood thick carpets of undulating forest and soon the trees in the forest became coated with white frost sparkling under the blue-veined moon as if it were icing sugar.

Sybil's wings shimmered in the starlight as she changed direction and began to descend closer to the earth. She could sense that she was almost home, but where was home?

Gradually she came to settle in a large snowdrift, beyond it Freddie could see the glimmer of faint light coming from a building set amongst tall pines. Sybil shook herself and the three travellers fell from her back into the snow. Humphrey's teeth chattered, he wished, not for the first time, that he had remembered to wear a scarf and hat, but then Sybil hadn't really given him time to think before trying to escape from him in his garden.

'What's that?' Katy pointed to the flickering glow framed by the trees.

'I don't know,' Freddie answered, 'but I think we should take a look. Mr. Entwhistle what do you think?'

Humphrey turned to the children, he was surprised they were asking him. After everything he had done he fully expected to be ignored by them. Sybil was less forgiving, her green eyes glared at him suspiciously, but then she slowly clambered out of the snow and began to amble towards the light.

'I don't think that we have any choice but to follow,' he replied. His lips were blue with cold and so numb that he found it difficult to form words. 'We don't know where we are and we shouldn't really stay outside in this weather if we have the chance of shelter.'

They all looked to the light and began to stumble towards it. Sybil had melted into the trees, she was definitely becoming harder to see, and she looked almost as if she was dissolving into the snow, but something drew her on. Kate wondered where the dragon had brought them and the second question which went around in her brain was, how on earth were they going to get home?

Chapter 10. The Ice Palace

The trees towered above them, creaking in the wind as they pushed their way through the deep carpet of snow. Now and again there was a huge "plop" as snow slid and fell from the bowing branches. The children struggled to lift their feet at times where drifts had collected against tree trunks or in unseen ditches, and the warmth of the gleaming, amber light in front of them became more inviting, but seemed more inaccessible with each step. The smooth, pearly face of the skittish moon played hide and seek between the tree tops, reluctant to let the plodding travellers see her. With frozen fingers and aching legs the three wanderers finally floundered into a large clearing in the forest. Before them stood a palace made of what looked at first to be ice. It shimmered and sparkled silver in the starlight and beyond the windows they could see dancing shadows thrown upon the walls by the flickering orange and yellow flames of something lit within.

'Hey,' said Freddie through frozen lips, 'It's your snow globe!'

Sure enough, the palace was exactly like the one in Katy's snow globe. Its turrets shone like white ghostly fingers prodding the scudding violet clouds, and above huge stone steps two great wooden doors were slightly ajar as if waiting for unexpected guests. As they came closer they realised that the walls of the palace were not ice, but made of a translucent stone. Upon the doors of the entrance were engraved dragons, their scales inlaid with mother of pearl and from their mouths the carpenter had fashioned rolling icy breath forming into icicles hanging from carved trees and casting snow over wooden dwelling places. At the top of the steps stood Sybil. She looked at Katy beseeching her to follow, the flames from beyond the doors reflected in her body seemed to be setting her alight, and yet almost shrouded her entirely from sight. Then with a quiver of her tail Sybil vanished, slipping between the doors and into the palace.

They all stopped and glanced at one another. The warmth and light filtering through the open doors beckoned to them invitingly, but still they hesitated even though the chill wind whistled about them, turning their eyelashes thick with icy crystals and their ears and noses pink with cold.

Suddenly there was a loud sneeze which so startled Katy she practically jumped three feet into the air. Freddie grabbed her arm and Humphrey Entwhistle's eyes bulged even more than usual in fright. They turned in the direction of the noise and noticed something they had missed before, to one side of the steps leading to the great doors stood a glistening pine tree, different to all the others. Although its branches were covered in snow, hanging upon it were lavender blue pine cones edged in silver, just like the one growing in Grandpa Ron's garden. Beneath it sat two deer, their antlers shining with light, their great moist eyes staring at the children and Humphrey.

'Ahhh ..... I see you have met Elding and Bruma, my tree guardians.'

At first Katy thought that the voice was coming from the deer, but no. Someone stood at the top of the stairway at the entrance of the palace. The glow behind the figure made it hard for them to see anything beyond a dark silhouette.

'Come in, come in. You received my message I can tell. I have been waiting for you. Your little dragon has come in and made herself known to me. Now I would like to introduce myself. I am Sigfrid and I wish to thank you for bringing her home. You must be very tired and hungry, I wish to hear everything and then I shall tell you why you are here.'

'What should we do Mr Entwhistle?' whispered Katy. Humphrey wasn't used to having this sort of responsibility. He was used to looking after number one. But instead of being irritated by her question he considered it carefully, he supposed he owed the children something, after all they had stopped him from falling off the dragon's back.

'I don't think that we have any choice Katy. It's far too cold to stay outside for long and we need to find a way to get home again at some point,' he whispered back to her.

Humphrey climbed the steps with the children following him. The dark figure of Sigfrid disappeared beyond the doors and when Katy and Freddie reached the top they could see into a huge hallway. They were surprised to feel the floor beneath them warm and yet there was no fire lit anywhere. The glow they had seen was from the torches held by beautifully wrought sconces along the great walls. On a huge rug lay Sybil, weary from her flight and having to carry three passengers, she dozed contentedly and Katy realised with a twinge of dismay that this was indeed where Sybil was really meant to be. Instinct had drawn her ever northwards, Sigfrid had foreseen she would arrive and this was now her home. They all looked at him curiously in the bright torch light. He had a thick white beard which spread down to his chest and his curly white hair was tied at the nape. The jerkin he wore was red, heavily embroidered with snowflake crystals, on his feet were boots laced up to the knee and on his arms circlets of gold flashed and chinked as he moved.

Freddie cleared his throat slightly nervously and spoke to him.

'Excuse me sir,' (his mum had always taught him to be polite) 'but were you expecting us?'

'Please, sit first and make yourselves comfortable,' their strange host replied. He pointed to a long table, surrounded by a number of high backed chairs, the mellow wood of which glowed warm in the torchlight. Upon it stood four steaming silver goblets and next to them a plate piled high with what looked like dainty biscuits.

'Yes, I was expecting you,' Sigfrid replied once they were all sat at the table. 'You must have seen my message soon after finding Sybil.'

'Message?' Katy frowned as she nibbled on one of the delicious wafers. 'I don't remember a message.' As she swallowed the wafer it sank down into her stomach gently warming her whole body. She sniffed at the steaming goblet in front of her, it smelt of chocolate and cinnamon, so she took a sip.

Freddie grinned at her and then at Sigfrid. 'You mean the snow globe don't you?'

'Yes,' Sigfrid nodded, his eyes shone in amusement. 'Yes, when I realised the ice tree was missing I knew we had to find it quickly. If it fell into the wrong hands your little dragon would be captured and great harm could have been done.' With this he turned to Humphrey and looked at him very sternly. Humphrey blushed red and looked very embarrassed, he felt Sigfrid looked right down into the depths of his soul and didn't approve of it very much!

'The ice and snow dragons keep balance in the world, bringing the cold winds of the northern winter that nurture creatures who love the frozen wastes and forests. It is harder and harder to keep them safe as few lands are now unexplored and humans take what they need without thought or understanding. The ice trees are fragile and fewer ice dragons are born, but they are needed now more than ever. Children, how many winters have you known snow in your county of red earth?'

'Not many,' answered Freddie shaking his head. 'Our winters are getting warmer, or so my grandad tells me.'

'Exactly, every ice dragon is precious. The message was for your little ice dragon, she eventually recognised it and her instincts did the rest.'

'But what I don't understand is who would have taken the tree in the first place?' Katy asked him.

'There are many who make mischief, some by mistake, and others with evil intentions. Trolls who live in the depths of the valleys and caves, men who plunder the earth for its riches and secrets because they believe they own it. The dragons are in danger from all of them.'

Sigfrid sighed. 'Each ice tree yields one dragon, the one in your grandfather's garden will not give up any more dragons, therefore we are very grateful that you have brought this one home to us.'

'But we didn't really do anything,' Katy explained. 'Sybil found her way here, we had no idea where to take her.'

'You nourished her and protected her. Then when her instincts told her what to do, you didn't stop her, you let her go. Now she will stay here with the rest of the ice dragons and do what she was born to do.'

'The rest?' queried Humphrey. He looked around rather apprehensively, he couldn't see any dragons except Sybil inside the enormous echoing hall.

'Yes, of course there are more and they will be here soon.' Sigfrid pointed to a window through which they could all now see brilliant colours rolling across the sky.

'Aurora Borealis,' murmured Humphrey.

'What?' Katy asked him.

'It's the northern lights, solar particles in the upper atmosphere collide with the different gases in it creating the colours,' he replied.

'Oh,' Katy had heard of this, but never really seen this strange and beautiful spectacle. Freddie was already eager to go outside to watch.

'Now we will meet the others,' Sigfrid said to them. 'Come.'

Katy and Freddie each took a handful of biscuits and popped them into their pockets as they left the table with Sigfrid nodding approvingly at them.

The carved palace doors opened to reveal a glorious sight. The sky danced in a gorgeous raiment of blues, greens, violets, yellows and pinks, lighting up the snow with its ethereal radiance. They all gasped in astonishment at the brilliant display, even more so when they realised that as the light hit the ground it flashed upon the scales of dozens of ice dragons as they stood in one gigantic circle around the palace. The two deer lying by the door sniffed the air and grunted, but apart from this were undisturbed - unlike Humphrey, Katy and Freddie who gazed in awe. The dragons were there one moment and gone the next. The scales which covered their bodies made them invisible until the light from the heavens bounced from them.

The children followed Sigfrid down the steps hesitantly at first, as these dragons were immense with coiled power. Katy knew that with one breath they could blow the palace and everyone near it miles away over the tops of the towering forest, into the vast ice and snow mists broiling at the top of the world. But then she felt a soft nuzzling at her hand and looked to see Sybil, who had come after them and now sat next to Katy reassuringly. Her great green eyes unblinking and steadfast.

All seemed strangely silent until Sigfrid raised his hand and spoke.

'My friends we have these three travellers to thank for the return of our newest dragon, whom our friends have named Sybil. This name she shall keep for all time. But this not the only reason that they have come here. For a long time we have known that another dragon keeper would be sent to us and now they have arrived.' Katy and Freddie looked at one another in consternation, what could Sigfrid mean?

'Thundersnow,' at this name one of the dragons raised their head. 'You must decide which of our visitors the chosen one is.'

Hope and terror battled in each of the three standing in the clearing.

'I really want to go home, but this could be the greatest adventure of all,' each thought to themselves.

The dragon named Thundersnow walked ponderously towards them, his great feet left enormous imprints in the snow, nevertheless he moved almost soundlessly until he reached the small group in front of him. His eyes swept over them all and then fixed on one person, his head bowed before them as he crouched there. He had chosen.

Katy felt her heart sink. When she looked across at Freddie she could see her own disappointment mirrored in his face, not only that but there was also disbelief.

Humphrey's own look was one of amazement as the huge dragon lay at his feet.

Sigfrid seemed to sense their incredulity.

'I cannot always understand the ways of the dragons, but they know best. They can take the dullest metal and fashion it into the truest and sharpest tool for good.'

Katy wasn't sure how Humphrey might feel about being chosen especially as "dull metal", would he even agree to stay here in the wilds of the cold north?

Humphrey himself was wondering the same thing. He may have travelled the world and faced some dangers, (as few as possible obviously) but his goal had always been to be a 'celebrity'. He realised no one could know about it if he stayed, there would be no TV interviews, no lucrative book deals, no press dogging his heels, nothing to advertise his new life.

But what would he gain? A unique place in the world? Certainly not fame he could enjoy, he would now be one of those explorers who had disappeared without trace.

Sigfrid's voice broke into his thoughts. 'Well, do you accept?' he asked Humphrey.

Humphrey was surprised to find himself nodding in agreement, he suddenly felt very sure as his eyes skimmed over the clan of dragons bathed in the northern lights. Despite Sybil's distrustful looks and the fact that his thermal underwear had now become unbearably itchy Humphrey Entwhistle was now certain he would stay with the ice dragons.

'Now, children it is time for you to return home, I regret that your stay here has had to be so short. We can never thank you enough for all that you have done, you already know that you can say nothing of this to anyone, ever.' Sigfrid beckoned to one slightly smaller ice dragon.

'Hoarfrost here is one of our swiftest dragons on the wing. So fast in fact that no one will realise you have been away for very long at all, as time will go backwards. I am grieved to tell you that when next a clock strikes midnight you and anyone else concerned with finding Sybil will forget everything that has happened, you will only remember what you need to, so say your goodbyes now.'

Katy clasped Sybil around the neck and buried her face into her, sorrowful tears started to roll down, freezing to her eyelashes almost immediately.

Freddie meanwhile solemnly shook Humphrey's hand, not because he particularly liked him, but it just seemed the right thing to do.

'Do not worry we will take care of her,' Sigfrid added kindly to Katy as she sat astride Hoarfrost with Freddie. '*She* will not forget *you*, I can promise that.'

With strongly beating wings Hoarfrost rose into the air. Sigfrid, Humphrey and Sybil shrank to become small black dots far, far beneath them. The cloak of invisibility all adult ice dragons seemed to have was complete, anyone looking up into the night sky would have seen the moon and stars as usual, and only heard a rush of wind as the dragon streaked past. It wasn't long before the children realised that in fact their journey with Sybil had indeed been a lot slower and must have taken all her strength to do.

Hoarfrost on the other hand with her powerful speed devoured the miles that lay between the frozen north and the red cliffs of Devon effortlessly. Ice flows, snowy mountains, and gloomy forests gave way to the sparkling lights of villages and towns in what seemed like the twinkling of an eye. And when the dragon alighted in the car park of the church and the children had thanked her for bringing them home, people were only just starting to emerge from the doors.

No one saw the dragon of course, but Katy's grandparents and Freddie's sister Amy soon spotted them.

'Where've you been?' demanded Amy indignantly. 'I was looking for you, Miss Hubbard let me be an angel in the nativity with wings and everything,' she added proudly. Katy's grandparents glanced at her enquiringly, as Professor von Flusspferd had attempted to explain to them and Freddie's parents that they'd had to leave, but would be back soon, leaving out any mention of dragons of course.

Unseen by anyone, Hoarfrost launched herself once more back into the night sky to return home. The icy draught from her wings caused people to pull their coats tighter around them and pull their hats further down over their ears. Winston and Charlie shivering, said they hoped that there would be ginger punch to warm the cockles when they arrived back at Whispering Pines and Amy was desperate to go home as she wanted to make sure that there were enough carrots left in the fridge to give to Father Christmas's reindeer.

They all wished each other a "Merry Christmas" and

got into their cars and minibuses to wend their way home. But not before Freddie had pressed a small package into Katy's hand.

'What's this?' asked Katy.

'Your Christmas present.' Freddie replied.

'But yours is at home Freddie, I forgot to bring it with me.'

'That's OK, I'll probably see you tomorrow anyway. Merry Christmas!' he grinned at her.

Katy closed her eyes as they rode back in the car. She felt exhausted and a little sad. What had Sigfrid said to them as they had left? They would only remember what they had to? What did that mean?

As they drew up to the gates of the house she realised that her parents' car was parked outside. But surely they were early? And as they opened the front door first her mum, then her dad rushed to greet them. They were also bursting with the news that the police had been around asking where the owner of the house next door was, as some curious noises had been reported coming from the garden, where eventually poor Marjory Farthing had been found and released from the cage.

'Where's Ruthie?' Katy looked beyond them into the hallway.

'Here I am!' said the voice of her sister. And there indeed she was, in the sitting room under the shimmering tree like a long awaited Christmas present.

'Katy everything is going to be OK, the doctors are really pleased. They say I should be able to dance again without much problem.' She brimmed with excitement and happiness as she hugged Katy to her.

The decorated tree looked beautiful in the firelight and smelt of pine forests far away in the north. Above the crackling logs in the fireplace on the mantelpiece sat the snow globe knowingly glinting in the candlelight.

By the time they had eaten supper, chatted and listened to carols it was very late. Katy went up to her bedroom and looked out of the window. In the distance she heard the clock starting to chime midnight. Softly snowflakes began to drift down from the dark, night clouds settling on Grandpa Ron's garden. They fell on the bird table, they fell on the shed and they fell onto the silvery-blue cones of the mysterious magical tree, whispering their soon to be forgotten secrets.

Katy felt in the pocket of her trousers. There was the gift Freddie had given to her, wrapped in gold tissue paper. She opened it slowly, after all it was Christmas Day now. The tissue fell to the floor and there in her hand was a dainty pendant he had made for her at school.

As the last stroke of midnight rent the air and before the memory was taken from her, she saw that on it he had painted a tiny ice dragon.

Books By This Author

The Moon Gardens

A wicked enchantress seeks to regain her magic power through the theft of a precious gemstone.

Standing in her way are a wise elder and his two apprentices from the 'Knoll'. Helped by Valerian of the Coral Caves, an owl and a magpie they set off on an exciting quest through enchanted mountains, plains and forests in a valiant attempt to avert disaster.

Can they reach the Moon Gardens in time or will the mysteries, deceits and disguises they encounter on their way foil them and bring ruin to the world they know.

Printed in Great Britain
by Amazon